Heartbreak

Lily craned her slender neck, scanning the cafeteria for signs of the ominous, monstrous "crowd" that Roxanne had described. "Who exactly is in 'the crowd'?" she asked.

Roxanne pointed with one coral-colored fingernail. "They are," she said.

Lily looked where Roxanne was pointing. At a large round table in the corner she saw Frankie and her new boyfriend, and Karen, and . . . Lily's heart leaped and then fell. *Jonathan.*

"Oh," Lily said out loud. Inside, she thought dismally, Oh, Jonathan. She could have sworn she could feel her heart break. The boy whose gray eyes had sent stars flying into her own had turned out to be Public Enemy Number One!

#1 *Change of Hearts*
#2 *Fire and Ice*
#3 *Alone, Together*
#4 *Made for Each Other*
#5 *Moving Too Fast*
#6 *Crazy Love*
#7 *Sworn Enemies*
#8 *Making Promises*
#9 *Broken Hearts*
#10 *Secrets*
#11 *More Than Friends*
#12 *Bad Love*
#13 *Changing Partners*
#14 *Picture Perfect*
#15 *Coming on Strong*
#16 *Sweethearts*
#17 *Dance with Me*
#18 *Kiss and Run*
#19 *Show Some Emotion*
#20 *No Contest*
#21 *Teacher's Pet*
#22 *Slow Dancing*
#23 *Bye Bye Love*
#24 *Something New*
#25 *Love Exchange*
#26 *Head Over Heels*
#27 *Sweet and Sour*
#28 *Lovestruck*
#29 *Take Me Back*
#30 *Falling for You*
#31 *Prom Date*

Special Editions
Summer Heat!
Be Mine!
Beach Party!
Sealed with a Kiss!

Coming soon . . .

#32 *Playing Dirty*

PROM DATE

by M.E. Cooper

SCHOLASTIC INC.
New York Toronto London Auckland Sydney

ISBN 0-590-41266-3

 Published by Scholastic Inc. Cover Photo: Pat Hill;

12 11 10 9 8 7 6 5 4 3 2 1 8 9/8 0 1 2 3/9

Printed in the U.S.A. 01

First Scholastic printing, April 1988

Chapter 1

"Pull, pull! Come on, seniors, *harder*!" Jonathan Preston hollered. As student activities director at John F. Kennedy High School and chief organizer of the Kennedy High May Day Celebration, Jonathan was supposed to be an unbiased referee at the various games. He couldn't help cheering for his classmates, though, as they faced off against the juniors in the tug-of-war finals on the football field. The juniors had already soundly beaten the freshmen, and the seniors had squashed the sophomores. But this match was close.

Now, after taking off his hat and dropping it at his feet, Jonathan ran one hand rapidly through his light brown hair. With the other, he held a whistle to his lips, poised to signal the imminent victory of the senior class. Jonathan watched the faces of his senior friends as they strained to tug the juniors across the line of orange chalk. Eric Shriver was putting all his swimmer's muscles into the battle. Diana, Jeremy, Matt, Holly, Brian, and Karen were pulling hard, too. Everyone was really digging in with their sneakers. Even tiny Molly Ramirez had her hands on the rope — she was an aikido black belt and stronger than she looked. The dirt was flying. Jonathan was kind of glad Mr. Briggs, the football coach, wasn't around to see his field getting all dug up.

The juniors began to lose ground fast. Jonathan's eyes stayed glued to Greg Montgomery's scuffed docksiders. Greg was first on the junior side and despite his heroic efforts, his feet were being dragged perilously close to the orange line. Another yard . . . a few more inches. . . .

Jonathan let out a sharp blast on the whistle. The senior class dropped the rope. They jumped up and down, slapped hands and shouted, leaving the juniors to tumble into a defeated pile. Jonathan didn't stay to congratulate the winners. Instead, he grabbed his hat and, tucking the whistle into the front pocket of his baggy khaki trousers, hurried with long, lanky strides across campus to the main quad where most of the May Day action was taking place. The water-balloon toss was due to start in a few minutes, as well as the three-legged race and the giant tricycle relay. . . .

Jonathan heaved a sigh. Sometimes he wondered why he got himself into so many projects. Forget getting himself into them — he dreamed them up and ran them from start to finish! Well, he liked being involved, that was all. In his community, at school. . . . It was an important part of his life. But lately he knew he'd been getting *too* involved. He'd been driving himself like a maniac all spring, managing one school event after another. With all the time he'd put in on the May Day Celebration, he hadn't seen much of his friends lately. He'd hardly even been able to keep up with his schoolwork. He wasn't too worried, though. He'd graduate all right, and he had a place waiting in the freshman class at U Penn in the fall.

Graduation. It was coming up fast. That was part of it, Jonathan told himself. He wouldn't be student activities director at Kennedy for much longer. He wouldn't be *anything* at Kennedy much longer. He had to use up his enthusiasm for his school in the weeks that were left. But even as Jonathan was silently analyzing the motives behind his recent burst of energy, he knew he wasn't being entirely honest with himself. There were other reasons. . . .

He entered the quad. The fresh spring breeze stirred the leaves of the now blossomless cherry trees and caused the colorful May Day banners to flap wildly. A moment later, Jeremy Stone had caught up with him and was slapping him on the back. Jeremy's pin-striped shirt was damp from the tug-of-war match. "So, Preston!" he greeted his friend. His soft British accent had become much less pronounced during the time he'd lived in the United States. "What craziness is next? The air band contest?"

Jonathan turned to find the whole gang catching up with him. Molly reached up to lift her dark brown ponytail off the back of her neck and smiled playfully at Jeremy. "Where've you been,

Jeremy? They did that ages ago, before the tug-of-war!" Her blue eyes crinkled at the corners. "It was an all-star show, too. The Pretenders and Bruce Springsteen and the E Street Band put up a good fight, but Tom Petty and the Heartbreakers won it."

Jeremy had taken Diana Einerson's hand and was swinging it lightly. "I guess we missed it," he acknowledged. He glanced down ruefully at the grass-stained knees of his gray trousers. "We arrived just in time to get dragged through the dirt."

"Being part of the action can get messy," his blonde girlfriend teased. She knew — and so did everyone else — that Jeremy preferred watching the action from behind the lens of one of his many cameras, video or otherwise.

"And if you hang around awhile longer, you can get even dirtier," Jonathan promised him cheerfully. "There are a lot more fun and games to come." He checked his watch and then looked around him. It didn't look as if May Day would stop in its tracks if he took a break for a few minutes. "What do you say, gang?" he asked as he dropped to the grass. "Take ten?"

Seconds later the whole group was sprawled in a loose circle alongside Jonathan. Everyone except Molly, who had dashed off to the refreshment table to return with an armful of sodas and a paper plate piled with homemade muffins. "Coffee, tea, or me?" she joked, tossing an icy can of Diet Coke in Eric's direction.

"Thanks, but I'll just stick with this." He

fielded the can with one hand and waved at her with a grin.

Molly laughed and sat down next to him, her legs folded Indian-style. She popped open a can of Slice for herself and held it out toward Jonathan. "Here's to another great Kennedy High extravaganza," she toasted, "courtesy of Jonathan Preston!"

"Hear, hear," his friends chorused.

"Hey, everybody helped." Jonathan refused to take full credit. "Don't blame me!"

"Still," Molly insisted, reaching for a blueberry muffin, "without you, Kennedy wouldn't have half the activities it does, and you know it."

The group nodded in agreement. The same thought seemed to be mirrored on all nine faces: With graduation a little more than a month away, there wouldn't be that many more occasions like this — not just special school events like fairs and fund-raisers, but ordinary old times to be together. Soon, the crowd would be split up as each person went his or her own way to college or jobs. Knowing this made the friends appreciate the moments they had left together that much more.

Holly Daniels leaned over and tugged on her best friend Diana's long blonde braid. "Hey, Di, remember that time we were roller-skating to raise money for Garfield House, and you fell down right on top of. . . ?"

In an instant the whole crowd joined in with their favorite memories. Each person had a story to contribute that was funnier than the last.

Jonathan laughed as hard as the others at these recollections, but he couldn't help noticing that a lot of them were slightly edited — for his benefit. No one, not even her brother, Jeremy, mentioned Fiona Stone, Jonathan's former girlfriend. Fiona had been just as much a part of the crowd as Jonathan himself until she moved back to England to study ballet last winter. Before she left, she and Jonathan had broken up — painfully and, on his side at least, bitterly. Since then he'd learned to see their breakup as inevitable — their feelings for each other had never had a firm base in shared interests, or even shared opinions — but the subject of Fiona was still a sensitive one. Still, Jonathan would have preferred it if his friends would just mention her name now and then instead of leaving her out of every story to spare his feelings. It made it seem like Fiona and their times together, good and bad, had never even existed.

Jonathan shook his head to clear it. He tuned back into the conversation just as Matt Jacobson, his Adidas T-shirt exposing a sunburned neck from the afternoons he spent working at his uncle's gas station, threw a handful of grass at a grinning Eric Shriver. "Yeah, Shriver, I remember the Valentine's Day Dance," Matt was reminiscing, a sheepish smile on his face. "It wasn't that long ago! And anyhow" — he raised a thick, dark eyebrow in Jonathan's direction — "I wasn't the only hopelessly romantic guy she bamboozled!"

Jonathan was already jumping to his feet, eager to get away from this conversation as rapidly and casually as possible. "Time to start tossin' those water balloons!" he declared quickly. "Don't forget the Ms. and Mr. America contest in half an hour." As he strode off, doing his best to appear purposeful, he could hear the gang still laughing over Matt's remark. Jonathan remembered Valentine's Day, too — all too well — but he had a hard time seeing it as a joke. His embarrassing stint with Roxanne Easton, a gorgeous junior who'd transferred to Kennedy midyear when nearby Stevenson High School was closed down, was still vivid in his mind. On the rebound from Fiona, Jonathan had rather heedlessly allowed the manipulative Roxanne to convince him that they were meant for each other. Not such a bad situation, except that she was pulling the *same stunt* with three of his best friends, Matt included. Rox's scheme was unveiled at the dance, where she'd arranged to have the special Valentine's Day computer date service pair her with all four guys. Jonathan had had an unpleasant surprise when he discovered he was sharing his dream girl four ways.

He smiled in spite of himself as he watched pairs of students tying their ankles together with bandannas in preparation for the three-legged race. Roxanne and Fiona — it would be hard to picture two more different girls. Fiona was beautiful but in a refined, delicate way. She was bright, determined, sharp, independent. Rox, on the other hand, was flashy, flirtatious, and altogether untrustworthy. *Fiona and Roxanne*. Between the two of them, they'd taught him a lot this year. Most of all, he'd learned that getting close to someone could be painful. He was better off steering clear of emotional attachments. It was safer to invest his energy in other things, like school activities. That way he couldn't get hurt again.

Whatever the reason for Jonathan's obsessive school spirit, he had to acknowledge that the result was a rousingly successful May Day Celebration. There was a huge turnout and everybody was having fun. Now it was time for what was sure to be the highlight of the day: the wacky, cross-dressed Ms. and Mr. America contest. The couples that entered had to dress like the opposite sex and do silly routines. The basic rule was anything goes, and dozens of kids were planning to participate. Dodging a few stray water balloons, Jonathan headed for the west corner of the quad where the Ms. and Mr. America hopefuls were gathering, some already in costume. Fortunately he wasn't judging this one — the winners would be chosen by a panel made up of three or four students and Principal Beman. Instead, Jonathan would be announcing each entry and keeping things running as smoothly as possible.

Moving through the milling crowd of students, Jonathan spotted a brown-haired girl holding a dry cleaner's plastic bag over one arm. "Hey, Elise," he called.

Elise stopped and turned toward him, her eyes sparkling in greeting. "Hi, Jonathan!"

He pointed at the bag she was holding. Multicolored cloth of some sort was visible through the transparent plastic. "You and Adam had better put your outfits on. They'll be starting any minute now."

Elise wrinkled her nose. " 'Fraid you're going to have to start without me. Adam had to cover the gymnastics meet for the newspaper at the last minute." She looked around hopefully. "I kind of thought he might make it back to school in time for the contest, but . . . I guess not." Elise was ready to shrug off her disappointment, but Jonathan wouldn't let her.

"You had a great act all planned," he protested. "You can't just waste it." He gripped Elise's arm with one hand and, shielding his eyes from the bright afternoon sun with the other, scanned the passersby for a potential partner for Elise.

"Really, Jonathan, it's okay," she assured him. "I'm just as happy to watch."

"Oh, no, you don't. Any guy here would love to sub as your Ms. America." He caught sight of a vaguely familiar face. It was Daniel Tackett, a transfer from Stevenson he'd talked to once or twice before. Jonathan didn't know much about Daniel, or any of the other Stevenson transfer students besides Roxanne, for that matter. He'd been too preoccupied with Fiona, and throwing all his energies into school events.

Elise watched as Jonathan collared Daniel and dragged him over to her. "Daniel, have you met Elise?" he asked in a hearty voice. "She's got these great costumes, and you two would be a cinch to win the Ms. and Mr. America contest if you get together. Nothing permanent, mind you," he joked. "Adam Tanner would not approve."

Jonathan paused and turned expectantly to Elise. She looked stunned. Daniel, meanwhile, appeared amused.

"Um, Jonathan, I'd rather not compete in the contest," Elise said. "I mean it." Jonathan was surprised at the cool note in her voice. She was usually so friendly. But the expression in her eyes now as she reluctantly glanced Daniel's way could only be described as hostile.

Daniel pushed a strand of shaggy dark hair off his forehead and smiled slyly. "Suit yourself."

"Well, hey. . . ." Jonathan stared at Elise and then at Daniel and then back at Elise. Finally he shrugged. "Suit yourself," he echoed, his tone amiable. It occurred to him that Elise's unwillingness to be paired with Daniel might have something to do with the fact that he was from Stevenson. Earlier in the semester, there had been a lot of tension between the Kennedy crowd and the new kids from their former rival high school. The tension, which wasn't helped by the fact that half the Kennedy guys had fallen under Rox Easton's spell, had become even worse after Kennedy's star gymnast, Katie Crawford, broke her leg on the school ski trip in January. Despite the crowd's initial intention to welcome the transferees to Kennedy, the passing months only seemed to widen the gap between the Kennedy and Stevenson groups. As for the latest gossip, Jonathan couldn't say. Maybe he *had* heard something to do with Daniel Tackett recently — something about a newspaper article? He wasn't quite sure.

Since the fiasco with Roxanne, he'd been keeping his distance from the feud. He was embarrassed about the part he'd played in that particular chapter and wasn't eager for a repeat performance.

Now Jonathan nodded at Elise and at Daniel, or rather at Daniel's back, since he'd already started to swagger off, and breezed on. This time he ran into Jeremy and Diana. They had their heads close together, obviously conspiring. Looking up, Jeremy slung an arm around Jonathan's shoulders and pulled him into the huddle.

"My good man, what seems to be the problem?" Jonathan asked in a fair imitation of Jeremy's accent. Diana giggled.

"We want to enter the cross-dressing contest," Jeremy explained. "We hadn't planned on it, so we don't have costumes, but we've come up with a smashing idea. All we need is a hat. . . ."

Jonathan generously held out his fedora. Diana shook her head. "Not just *any* hat," she corrected, laughing as Jonathan pretended to look hurt. "We want a big straw hat with plastic fruit on it. Something kind of crazy . . . you know, like the Chiquita banana lady. For Jeremy!"

Jonathan narrowed his eyes, thinking. Then he shook his finger decisively. "I've got it!" he declared. "The costume room at the Little Theater! You guys stay here while I run over to check it. I'll be back in a minute."

Two minutes after leaving Jeremy and Diana, Jonathan was rushing through the door of the old colonial chapel, which had been renovated and turned into a theater. He trotted down the aisle and hopped onto the stage, pushing his way through the musty velvet curtains. Backstage, he took a left. Through the gloom at the end of a short hallway he could read the lettering on a dark green door: COSTUMES.

The door was ajar, but Jonathan didn't pause to wonder why. He stepped inside. Lined up on the floor underneath a tall rack in the center of the room were boxes of accessories labeled: SHOES, BELTS, GLOVES, etc. But the hats were scattered everywhere: on shelves, pinned to costumes. . . . Jonathan hardly knew where to start looking. The rack was as good a place as any, he decided, hurriedly flinging aside costume pieces. There was a Henry VIII-style tunic, tights, and tam — probably not what ol' Jer had in mind, he thought with amusement. Big Chief Somebody or Other with a feathered headdress? Naw. Jonathan was so busy searching for the right hat that he hardly noticed when his own hat tumbled off his head and into a box of assorted fishnet stockings. He was also too busy to notice for a full thirty seconds that he wasn't alone in the room. A sudden movement on the other side of the rack stopped him in his tracks. He bit back a yelp of surprise and then, his curiosity getting the better of him, he peeked through the clothes to the other side.

It was a girl . . . a girl he'd never seen before. She was standing with her back to him, facing a dusty full-length mirror on the opposite wall. She had picked up a hat and was trying it on, making funny faces at her reflection. For a moment, Jonathan was spellbound. The girl's face was thin and pale but pretty. As he watched, it seemed as if a thousand expressions flashed in her enormous, deep blue eyes. Her wide cheekbones narrowed to a waiflike, pointy chin. As she started to put the hat on, Jonathan suddenly recognized it. "Hey, that's *my* hat!" he shouted. He lunged forward through the costumes to swipe his fedora off the girl's head. She whirled around, staring at him with eyes made even wider by astonishment.

"That's my hat," he repeated, aware of how loud his voice sounded as it bounced off the walls of the cavernous room. "If you're looking for something to wear in the Ms. and Mr. America contest," he added briskly, "it can't be this."

The girl raised her slender, fair eyebrows. "I don't want it for the contest, I want it for the spring musical," she said, as if that explained everything.

Jonathan placed the fedora firmly back on his head. He was still leaning precariously through the rack of clothes, half-entangled in costumes. "Well, sorry," he said, pulling back to renew his search.

"But it would be perfect," the girl insisted. Before he could back away, she had snatched the fedora again. "Really, it's just what I'm looking for!"

"Once again, I'm sorry." Jonathan was entirely flustered. "You can't use it."

"I found it right here in the box." She pointed at the carton in question with a mischievous half-smile. "Finders, keepers, isn't that so?"

"No, that isn't so." Jonathan was very close to

losing his temper now. "It's my hat and I'd like it back!"

"I think I should get to keep it," she argued good-naturedly.

"It's mine," Jonathan fumed.

"Mine."

"*Mine!*"

The girl had been speaking in a light-hearted tone, but now her expression changed. "It's my hat and I'm holding on to it. Scram!" she commanded in a comically deep voice. She waved her arms at Jonathan and then yanked the fedora down over her eyes with a dramatic flourish. Jonathan's jaw dropped. The exaggerated glare she was directing his way was a perfect imitation of the impatient frown he could feel on his own face. With a start he realized the girl was showing him a fun-house mirror image of himself — a crazed Jonathan too frazzled and hurried to listen or even smile. He must have looked pretty ridiculous barreling right through a rack of costumes to yell at her! Jonathan's frown dissolved. He laughed so hard, he had a tough time untangling himself from the folds of Henry VIII's velvet cape. The girl laughed, too.

"I'm sorry," Jonathan finally managed to say once he was standing clear of the costumes on the other side of the rack. "I must have sounded like a big crab! You can borrow the hat if you want."

The girl removed the fedora and studied it for a moment. "To tell you the truth, it's really not what I was looking for," she admitted, her blue eyes twinkling. "Here."

Jonathan took the hat from her small outstretched hand. "Thanks," he said, tipping it at her before putting it back on his head. They both turned to leave at the same instant, stepping on one another's toes. As Jonathan met her warm, smiling eyes and laughed again, it struck him that this was the first time he'd laughed, really sincerely, in a long while. This cute, goofy girl had somehow gotten past all his defenses and touched his funny bone. And he didn't even know her name!

She was a few steps ahead of Jonathan and already had her hand on the doorknob when he cleared his throat. "Hey, um, I'm Jonathan Preston. Uh, who. . . ?

She turned to face him again. "Lily Rorshack. It's nice to meet you, Jonathan."

"Are you really in the spring musical?" he asked, impressed.

"Yeah." She shrugged nonchalantly. "I'm playing the mute in *The Fantasticks.* It's a mime role. Do you know the play? It's really fun."

"Wow." Jonathan whistled. "Wow." Suddenly he couldn't think of anything else to say. Lily, too, seemed at a loss for words. They stood only a few inches apart, just inside the door that led back out to the stage. Jonathan stared at Lily and she stared back. Then they both laughed spontaneously. Lily reached for the door again, and this time she opened it.

She glanced back at Jonathan over one thin shoulder. "Well, I'll see you around."

The hopeful note in her voice inspired him. "You *will* see me," he assured her with a grin.

"I'll come cheer you on in *The Fantasticks*!"

Lily smiled shyly. "Great. Well, so long."

An instant later she had disappeared. Jonathan blinked, half in a daze. Was Lily for real or just the result of some freaky backstage magic? He bent his head forward and let his fedora drop into his hands. As he pictured her mugging in the mirror with his hat on, a slow smile spread across his face. Nope, Lily was for real all right. He was sure of it.

And speaking of hats! Jonathan had almost forgotten it was the middle of the May Day Celebration. The Ms. and Mr. America contest was probably over by now! As he dashed for the door, a flash of color caught his eye. There was a hat high up on a shelf to the right of the door.

Unbelievably, it was a wide straw sombrero decorated with plastic grapes, apples, and oranges. Maybe there was some magic in the air after all, Jonathan thought. Feeling really alive for the first time in months, he grabbed the hat and raced back out to the quad to find Diana and Jeremy.

Chapter 2

The following Monday, Greg Montgomery gave his locker a swift kick in the lower right-hand corner, and it bounced open with a clatter. Ever since he was assigned the locker on the first day of school his freshman year, that had been the only way to get it open. Usually it was just a pain in the neck, but sometimes — like today — it was a good way to release energy or vent his frustrations. Greg shuffled through a stack of notebooks until he came to a red folder that was a little less dog-eared than the others. Written across the top in bold black felt-tip was the word CAMPAIGN. Tucking the folder under one arm, he slammed the locker shut noisily. That was another one of the locker's idiosyncrasies — you couldn't just close it, you had to *slam* it. And today Greg took as much pleasure out of slamming the locker shut as he had from kicking it open.

Somehow these harmless acts of violence made him feel a little bit better.

He headed down the hall away from the cafeteria, then up the stairs to the second floor, sighing as he went. He was skipping lunch today to go to a meeting — a meeting he'd called, actually. He was about to formally declare his candidacy for student body president, and the meeting would be a good chance to see who was interested in helping to start the ball rolling on his campaign. Greg expected a lot of his friends to be there, seniors as well as juniors. Graduating seniors were allowed to help on campaigns even though only underclassmen would vote in the election.

Logically Greg knew he should be feeling really psyched. He knew he would make a strong, capable president, and the experience would add a lot to his senior year. Not only that, but this year Kennedy was making its presidential race as much like a national election as possible. Running would be half the fun. So why was he dragging his feet? All Greg knew was, although he usually came alive in the spring, he'd been like a zombie lately. Even crew — and so far the team was having a fantastic season — didn't excite him much. He just felt drained, emotionally empty. And the one person in the world who had the power to bring him back to life, to make him care, was the same person who'd caused his problem in the first place.

It had been months — three months to be exact — since it all started. His girlfriend, or rather his ex-girlfriend, Katie Crawford, had broken her leg during the ski trip to Mount Jackson, and Greg couldn't count the times he'd thought he would give almost anything to wipe that day from the history of the world. Katie had taken the accident so hard. She was a serious gymnast, the star of Kennedy's state-champion team, and breaking her leg almost surely meant losing her chance to compete during her last high school season. If only Katie had been able to accept that, if only she hadn't insisted on blaming the whole thing on Roxanne Easton, he thought. And on him. Even so, for a while he'd had high hopes that their relationship would make it. He had to be understanding, that was all. But just when things were looking up again, Katie's spirits had taken a turn for the worse and this time Greg couldn't reach her. She'd given in to her depression and started hanging around with Roxanne's low-life younger brother, Torrey. She let Torrey draw her into his childish, destructive pranks, and by then Greg had finally had enough. They hadn't spoken in weeks now, not since she and Torrey had unintentionally sabotaged The Potomac Fun Race Greg had entered and he'd told her off for acting like a vandal and a fool. If she couldn't help herself, then no one could.

Greg scuffed his Reeboks along the institutional beige hall carpeting. Maybe he'd been too harsh with her. No, he argued silently with conviction, that behavior wasn't Katie. It wasn't worthy of the girl he knew and loved, and he wouldn't have been doing her any favors by encouraging it. Even worse, he knew that deep inside Katie, too, had recognized the mistakes she was making. He'd heard through the grapevine — from Katie's best friend, Molly, actually — that Katie was back at gymnastics practice and becoming her old self again. As for him, he was ready to talk things over, desperate to, but Katie wouldn't come near him. Their situation had been awkward and painful for so long. Greg knew the reason time didn't make it any better was because he still cared for Katie. They'd stopped seeing each other, but that hadn't stopped him from loving her.

The spare classroom that had been designated as Greg's campaign headquarters — each candidate had a similar space — was around the next bend in the corridor. The door was closed. For a split second before Greg pushed it open, he imagined that Katie would be sitting on the other side, waiting to tell him that she wanted to help out with his campaign, to be friends again. The door swung wide when he pushed it, and Greg ran a hand nervously through his neatly-cut sandy-colored hair. Groups of students were scattered in small clusters around the room. All were familiar faces: Frankie Baker and Josh Ferguson, Karen Davis and Brian Pierson, Jeremy and Diana, Holly, Jonathan, Matt, Eric, Molly, and others. Even Roxanne, Greg observed wryly. She was the only ex-Stevenson student there besides Frankie. But no Katie. He swallowed his disappointment and tossed the group a casual wave.

"Hey," Jonathan called to Greg from where

he sat on the windowsill with Molly. "Didn't know you had so many friends, huh, Monty?"

"This is great," Greg agreed with a sincere grin.

"Well, don't get cocky," Molly warned him playfully. "We'll only *stay* your friends if you win this election!"

"First he has to make it at the convention," Jonathan reminded her. In keeping with the national election theme, the two final candidates for president would be chosen at a mock convention in three weeks. "The convention is the key," Jonathan went on, hopping down from the windowsill. He began to pace in front of the teacher's desk, where Greg had taken a seat and was looking on, clearly entertained. "It's too soon to say how many people are going to run, but there'll probably be a lot. Some people will be torn between two candidates. Once the field is narrowed to two after the convention, though, Greg will be a shoo-in! So — "

"*So*, in case you haven't figured it out yet," Greg interrupted, "Jonathan's my campaign manager!" The crowd laughed noisily.

Jonathan lifted his hands, palms-up, and shrugged sheepishly. "What can I say. I'm gung ho. And you know, Monty, that's an important quality in a campaign manager. An enthusiastic campaign manager can — "

"Sit down!" Greg yelled politely. Jonathan returned to the window, grinning. A few of the others applauded. Eric threw an airplane made out of a brown paper lunch bag.

"Anyway, as you already know," Greg continued more seriously, "I called this meeting to formally announce that I'm running for student body president for next year." There was more clapping. Matt let out a piercing whistle, and from the back row Roxanne fluttered her thick eyelashes admiringly. Greg leaned forward, resting his elbows on the desktop. "Before we get into the details of campaigning, though, I thought I'd just say some things about how I feel about running for office; why I think it will be a good thing for Kennedy, and for me." Greg closed his eyes for a second, wrinkling his forehead thoughtfully. When he opened them again, he was smiling wryly. "To tell the truth, I'm looking forward to hearing this myself! I haven't really had much of a chance to put my thoughts on this into words. You'll have to let me know what you think when I'm done. At some point, I'm going to have to pull a convention speech out of all this."

Greg tipped his chair back, put his hands behind his head, and spoke for about five minutes. His friends were quiet and attentive. He knew that for all their clowning, they believed in him and would support him all the way. And he had confidence in himself. All the same, as he listened to his own words, he felt in a way as if he were listening to a stranger. He heard a quieter, more serious guy talking — the usual Greg Montgomery playfulness was missing. Well, whatever his mood, he planned to put everything he had into his campaign. Maybe becoming ultra-absorbed in something other than his breakup with Katie would bring some of the zip back into his life.

After Greg wrapped up his off-the-cuff speech, he asked his friends for their reactions. Discussion was lively, but after a few minutes he cut it short. "We only have fifteen minutes of lunch hour left," he announced, "and I don't want to keep you too long because everybody should eat. You've got to keep up your strength for this grueling campaign!"

As the rest of the crowd jostled toward the door after giving Greg handshakes and pats on the back, Jonathan hung around for a moment. "We'll have to have another meeting pretty soon, old pal," he advised Greg. "Just you and me. Plan some strategy."

"Yeah," Greg agreed, not really paying attention. His eyes were on the door, through which Molly, who'd been trailing the others, was about to disappear. "Let's talk about it later, okay?"

"Whatever you say." Jonathan winked. "You're the boss!"

Greg, meanwhile, had crossed quickly to the door. "Moll," he called, just as she stepped into the hallway. "Hold on a minute." She turned around, a questioning smile on her face. When she saw the somber look in Greg's gray-green eyes, she followed him back into the classroom.

"What is it, Greg?" she asked, concerned.

Greg waited until Jonathan had cruised past them and on into the hall, waving good-bye over his shoulder, and then said somewhat awkwardly, "Uh, Molly, did . . . did Katie know about this meeting? I mean about me running?"

For a second, before Molly replied, Greg let himself imagine that Katie hadn't known. She missed the meeting because she hadn't known, but when she found out, she'd be so excited for him. . . . She'd call him, maybe even stop by his house. She was graduating soon, but she'd want to leave Kennedy in good hands. They could work on the campaign together. . . .

Molly's first word shattered Greg's daydream. "Yes," she confessed apologetically. "She did know. I told her about it myself. I really hoped she'd want to come — "

"But . . ." Greg interjected dully.

"But she didn't," Molly finished. Her hands had been pushed deep in the pockets of her baby blue overalls. "I'm sorry."

"Hey, that's okay." Greg did his best to sound lighthearted. "I guess I'm not that surprised."

Molly shifted her weight from one foot to the other. She seemed uncomfortable, and Greg didn't want to put her on the spot by making her talk about her best friend behind her back. "Don't let me keep you," he said, nodding at the door.

"Do you want to come with me to the cafeteria?" Molly invited. "We still have time to grab a sandwich."

Greg shook his head. He really didn't feel like being sociable. "No, thanks. You go ahead. I'm going to stay here for a few more minutes." He gestured vaguely at the desk where his campaign folder was still lying open. "Maybe make a few more notes for my speech."

Molly's eyes were warm with sympathy. "Catch you later, then."

" 'Bye, Moll."

Greg strolled slowly back to the desk. He leaned against it, facing the empty classroom, his long legs stretched out in front of him and his arms folded across his chest. He bent his head and willed his mind to become a blank. He wished he could erase it, like the blackboard behind him, just wipe it clean of thoughts of Katie so he could concentrate on something else: crew, his campaign, anything. But he didn't have the mental energy. Since hearing that Katie skipped the meeting intentionally, he felt more weighed down than ever. With every day that passed that they didn't exchange a single word, the distance between them doubled. Soon they'd be complete strangers. The brief but intense past they'd shared might as well have never happened.

Greg ran a hand through his hair. Clenching his teeth with determination, he straightened up and walked around to the blackboard. When he scratched the stub of chalk across the board, however, instead of a list of campaign goals he saw that he had written Katie's name.

Grabbing the dusty eraser, he wiped the word away with one stroke just as a husky, feminine voice greeted him from the doorway. "Hi, there, Mr. President! How's tricks in the Oval Office?"

Greg froze, his hand still raised. He'd recognize that voice anywhere, "Hi, Roxanne," he said, replacing the eraser carefully and managing a polite smile.

Roxanne didn't seem to notice his stiffness. She breezed into the room, deposited her black snakeskin shoulder bag on the nearest chair and slid close to Greg, turning on the famous Rox Easton purr. It was all Greg could do to hold his ground. All his instincts were saying, "Run for your life!"

"I really enjoyed the meeting just now," Rox said breathily. The smile that accompanied her words was calculated to melt ice, but Greg had seen it before, and he knew what lay behind it. Roxanne's beauty didn't much affect him anymore. As he settled back against the desk, cornered, Greg couldn't help recalling the first time Roxanne had tried that smile on him. He'd fallen for her looks and her lines like a ton of bricks, just like every other guy at Kennedy. Greg had finally wised up to her deceitful ways . . . but it wasn't easy to keep fighting her back.

"I think you'll be a fabulous president," Rox was saying now. She tossed her mane of long, tawny hair from one side to the other to emphasize her statement. "I can't wait to help out with your campaign!" She lowered her lashes suggestively. "I'll do *anything* you want."

"That's nice, Roxanne," Greg said, taking a step away from her. Her perfume and her personality were both overpowering.

"You know, it's been a while since we had a chance to talk," Rox observed, leaning close again. "I don't think I've even seen you since . . . since the Potomac River Fun Race."

Roxanne's dark green eyes were wide and innocent. Greg groaned inwardly at the reminder. The race had been a disaster! It all started when Torrey Easton, Rox's brother, who was standing at the river's edge with Katie, began hollering insults at his sister, who was Greg's sailing partner in the race. Katie and Torrey then stole a rowboat and paddled out to the *Sally Ride II*, and by the time it was all over, both Greg and Katie had landed in the river. Katie, with her weak leg, had been forced to swim ashore. And ever since that day, she had been too ashamed of her jealous actions to even talk to him. Greg knew there was no doubt about it: Every time he got involved with Rox Easton in any way, it resulted in an awful mess, especially where Katie was concerned. The last thing he needed was for her to bulldoze her way into helping him with his campaign. That would be one surefire way to make certain Katie kept her distance.

He opened his mouth to say something that might encourage Rox to leave, but she was still chattering on, unperturbed by Greg's lack of response. "That race was a lot of fun, until the end, at least." She placed a hand on his arm and gave it a squeeze. Greg flinched. "I love sailing — especially with *you*."

Rox waited expectantly. "Er, me, too," Greg muttered. It was half true, anyway. He loved sailing, too.

"We should get together real soon," she pressed, her eyes warm with meaning.

It was all Greg could do to keep a straight face. The junior-senior prom was coming up in a few weeks, and Roxanne might as well have had the words "Ask Me" tattooed on her forehead. He knew she wasn't dating anybody, and she had to be very aware of the fact that his relationship with Katie was permanently stalled. Well, she could drop as many hints as she wanted. He wasn't picking up on any of them.

Standing up abruptly, he walked around to the other side of the desk, putting it between them. "Look Rox, I really need to work on my ideas for the campaign." He flipped purposefully through his notebook, hoping she wouldn't see the blank pages.

"Well, that's why I'm here!" Rox declared brightly. "I can be a big help, I *know* I can. My mother has connections with a political ad agency now, and I can get all sorts of great stuff through her." Her eyes sparkled with inspiration. "I could flood the campus with professional-looking buttons, posters, bumper stickers — you name it! It'd really make you stand out from the crowd. I mean, even more than you already do," she amended.

Greg scowled. "I don't want to buy the election," he said bluntly. "I want to win on my own merit." Roxanne's face fell, and Greg immediately regretted sounding so ungrateful. His voice softened slightly. "Thanks for the offer, though."

Roxanne took Greg's kinder tone as encouragement. "Well, there are probably other ways I can help, right?" She didn't give him a chance to contradict her. "Maybe I can come over some night and we can discuss them." Her smile promised a lot more than campaign advice.

Greg gulped. Roxanne might be nasty, but she was also incredibly sexy. "Well . . . we'll see," he said in his coolest voice.

Rox tossed her head. There was just the tiniest

trace of irritation in her voice when she renewed the attack. "But Greg, with me working with you on the campaign, you'll be sure to get the Stevenson vote," she argued, sweetly but insistently. "They'll support you if I tell them to. That could make a big difference."

Greg lifted his hands helplessly. He was holding on to his patience by a slim thread. "Rox, like I said — thanks, but it's all right. I think I can make it without scare tactics."

Roxanne frowned. She looked as if she were about to snap, but then, instead, she smiled. "But we're still on for the . . . for a night out together sometime, aren't we?"

Greg slammed his hands down on the desk. The smack echoed loudly in the empty classroom. "Look, Roxanne!" he burst out. "Read my lips. I'm not taking anyone to the prom. *Anyone.* And I don't want your help on my campaign. Understand?"

Roxanne's whole face had gone pale, right down to her lightly glossed lips. When she spoke, her voice shook with fury. "So, you don't want my help." She narrowed her catlike eyes. If looks could kill, Greg thought. "You Kennedy snobs think you're too good for the rest of the world! Well, you're about to find out otherwise."

With that, Roxanne whirled on the heels of her black ankle-strap sandals and stormed across the room, her ruffled denim miniskirt flouncing angrily. When she slammed the door behind her, Greg bet they could feel the vibrations all over school.

"Whew!" he whistled, shaking his head in

amazement. That was one mad girl. For a moment, he wondered if maybe he'd gone too far. He pictured the look in Roxanne's eyes. He'd seen it before and he knew what it meant. Trouble. Rox Easton was on the warpath.

Katie adjusted her leotard, which was hiking up in the back, and then climbed carefully onto the balance beam. As she eased into a half-split, she thought of how she used to mount the beam with a flying leap, launching right into cartwheels and handsprings. Well, no more. Since the first time she'd stepped back into the gym after having her cast removed, it was like starting over. She had to take everything slowly and cautiously. Her newly healed leg was too weak to do anything else.

But at least I'm here, she thought, gritting her teeth as she paced the beam. It's a step — literally! — in the right direction. When she first injured her leg, she'd been devastated at the thought of missing gymnastics season altogether. She *had* missed a lot of it, true, but there were still a few meets left, and she planned to compete in all of them.

Katie dropped from her partial split to a sitting position on the beam and rested for a moment, massaging her ankle thoughtfully. She recalled the day her cast had come off. She'd felt as light as a feather! All of a sudden the world had looked bright again, and she wondered how she could ever have been so discouraged, so negative. Why hadn't she been able to do what Greg had counseled her to do all along, hang on to that ray of hope that her leg would heal in time for gymnastics, see the positive side, make the best of things? Instead, she'd fallen apart at the seams. All her life she'd been a winner. Her achievement in gymnastics was the outward expression of what she considered the best part of herself. When it was taken away, she'd felt she'd lost everything.

Flipping her long red ponytail over her shoulder, Katie got to her feet again. This time she tried a front walkover. Easy does it . . . did it! she thought triumphantly. Now if she could only do it with more speed and bounce. She sighed. She didn't dare, not yet.

Katie paused at the end of the beam and glanced at her watch. Only ten more minutes of practice. Vaguely she wondered if there was any chance that she'd bump into Greg coming back from crew in the parking lot on her way out. Then she reminded herself that she didn't *want* to bump into him. In fact, she'd been doing her best lately to avoid him. She'd stayed away from his meeting that day at lunch even though all her friends went, and even though deep inside she was proud of Greg and would have liked to let him know that. She knew he'd been disappointed that she didn't show up — Molly admitted that to her during English. But she couldn't face him, or the whole presidential candidacy thing. Greg was a success story. Self-confidence glowed from within him. It was one of the things that had always made him so attractive to her. But now his confidence only reminded her how far her own self-esteem had dropped. Katie knew Greg wanted to talk and at least be friends, but until she felt as if she were on an equal footing with him, until *she* felt like a winner again, she just couldn't deal with him or with what might be left of their relationship.

Katie brushed her bangs off her forehead and tried to concentrate on the balance beam. In the past, she'd always gone all-out during the last few minutes of her practice, made her final routine of the day her best. Taking a deep breath, she took a few steps forward and then pivoted one hundred eighty degrees. Back walkover, back walkover. . . . In spite of her efforts, Katie's leg was unsteady and her balance was slightly off. She fell off the beam. That at least was nothing new — she'd fallen off the beam hundreds of times in her life. She couldn't let this fall discourage her any more than those others. She just had to pick herself up and try again.

Before Katie could remount the beam, her eye was caught by a flash of lime green. It was Stacy Morrison in her new leotard. The sophomore tumbled by on the neighboring floor mats, giggling as she went. At the end of her run she added a few cheerleading-style jumps just for fun. Katie raised an eyebrow. She could imagine what Coach Muldoon would have to say about that kind of fooling around!

Grabbing her towel off the chair by the beam, Katie paused for a moment to watch Stacy. She was the new hope for the team — Katie's injury and her upcoming graduation were leaving a big gap — but Stacy was a goof-off. She had terrific potential and natural talent to spare, but little technique or discipline. Katie thought of the countless hours *she'd* spent, from childhood on, working on each new movement until it was perfect. If Stacy had half that sort of dedication, Katie was sure she could be a star. But instead of practicing, Stacy played. Just then she abruptly left the mats, right in the middle of her floor routine. Katie watched her trot to the gym door where two cute Kennedy High baseball players were lounging. Flirting clearly interested her more than working out.

Katie shook her head in disgust. She felt like shouting at Stacy. Didn't she know that talent like hers was a gift? A precious, fragile gift? She should appreciate it, not waste it. You never knew when something might take it away.

But instead of shouting, Katie turned quietly to face the balance beam again. She'd give that back walkover one more shot.

Chapter 3

As Roxanne deposited her lunch tray at the table where she normally ate, the usual bitter taste was in her mouth. The so-called "Stevenson table," where her junior and senior friends from her old school sat, wasn't far from the Kennedy "in" crowd's preferred table in the north corner of the cafeteria. Every time Rox took her place at the Stevenson table, she burned because she wasn't sitting at the other one. She knew she wasn't welcome there.

Of course, it had been an entirely different story at first. During her first couple of weeks at Kennedy, she got loads of attention from the popular crowd, or at least the guys in the popular crowd. Greg, Eric, Matt, Jonathan — they had all been eating out of her hand. She was well on her way to a position of power in the Kennedy social structure. But something had gone wrong — Roxanne still wasn't sure exactly what — and all her ingenious plans had fallen apart. Since then she'd been getting the cold shoulder, pretty much all around. She'd thought she still might have a chance with Greg, who was by far the best-looking and most charismatic in the bunch. After the way he'd treated her last week after his campaign meeting, though. . . .

Rox barely greeted her tablemates. She was too busy scoping the crowd's table without appearing to do so. "Hi, Zack, hi, Daniel," she said absentmindedly.

Daniel Tackett shoved his chair back to sit with his feet on the table, one cowboy boot crossed over the other and his hands pushed into the pockets of his faded Levi's 501s. "Foxy Roxy," he greeted her, a lazy smile flickering across his sharp-featured, rugged, but attractive face. "How's the world treating you these days?"

Zachary McGraw inched over to make more room for Roxanne. Next to his tray, laden with two cheeseburgers, potato chips, and a piece of cherry pie, her own yogurt with fruit and granola looked pretty paltry. Oh, to be a football player, she thought enviously. Aloud, in answer to Daniel's question, she said, "Just fair, if you really want to know." Her pretty mouth curved into a pout. "If you *really* want to know," she went on, her voice rising indignantly, "I've had just about enough of the way things operate around here! Nothing's changed since the first day we transferred. Stevenson kids are still treated like second-class citizens. That crowd" — she nodded crisply in their direction — "is so uppity and exclusive. They won't let us get involved in anything important. It's *their* prom, *their* presidential election. And let me tell you, if that preppy snob Greg Montgomery wins for student body president, which he probably will, things will get even worse!" Roxanne concluded this tirade with a dramatic toss of her auburn hair.

Daniel rolled his eyes and the rest of the kids at the table exchanged knowing glances. The theme was familiar: No lunch hour would be complete without Roxanne bringing up "the crowd" and beating the subject into the ground. The transition from Stevenson to Kennedy had been hard for everybody, but no one seemed to have taken it more to heart than Roxanne.

"They're not all bad," Zachary protested, his bright blue eyes gentle.

"Oh, yeah?" Rox refrained from reminding Zack of how he'd been duped by Kennedy senior Holly Daniels, who from every report she'd heard, was now happily back together with her long-time boyfriend, Bart Einerson, a Kennedy graduate. But even innocent Zachary couldn't have missed Roxanne's insinuating tone. Underneath his track-season tan, his cheeks reddened slightly.

"I don't know, I sort of agree with Zack," Daniel said thoughtfully. "I'm not so sure they're all rotten to the core."

"Oh, come off it, Daniel!" Roxanne waved an impeccably manicured hand. "You know as well as I do that they've blackballed every Stevenson kid who's tried to get involved in anything. I mean, look at how they treated you at the newspaper! But I have a plan. . . ." She leaned toward him conspiratorially, her green eyes glinting.

"You'll run for student body president against Greg! I'll be your campaign manager. With the buttons and stuff I can get through my mother, we'll make Greg look like an amateur!"

"I don't think so, Rox. Student body prez isn't really my style." Daniel shook a rebellious lock of hair away from his eyes. "I'm a journalist, not a politician," he added dryly.

"Baloney," Roxanne sniffed. "You're a leader, that's what you are. You were a leader at Stevenson, and you should be a leader here. It's your right!" She tapped her spoon on her tray for emphasis. "Don't you see what they're keeping you from accomplishing?"

Daniel brought his chair down with a bang. "What I see more clearly is what I've kept from myself," he muttered, half under his breath.

Rox heard him and raised an eyebrow, puzzled. "What do you mean?"

His eyes were bland as they met hers. "The only thing I really wanted here at Kennedy was a position on the school paper," he stated baldly. "And you know as well as I do that's next to impossible now."

"Oh," she said, slightly deflated.

Earlier in the semester, Daniel had approached Karen Davis, the editor of Kennedy's newspaper, *The Red and the Gold*, about joining the staff. Believing Rox's bad report about the crowd, he'd started out on the defensive, expecting Karen to blow him off. When, not surprisingly, she and her boyfriend, Brian Pierson, WKND's manager and chief disc jockey, gave him a chilly reception, he decided to get back at them with a harmless prank. Harmless — or so he thought. He talked Lily Rorshack, an aspiring comic actress, into posing as a reformed street kid in an interview with Karen. He told Lily to think of it as an "exercise" in acting. Karen had fallen hook, line, and sinker for Lily's hard-luck story. Not only had she printed the interview in *The Red and the Gold*, but she'd submitted it to a high school journalism contest sponsored by Georgetown University.

When the article first appeared in the paper, Daniel had been gleeful. Lily's fake interview was an inside joke with all the Stevenson kids; everyone played along with it. Rox had convinced them all that the Kennedy kids were stuck-up snobs; they deserved some razzing. But entering it in a contest was another matter altogether. Daniel, as an editor himself, knew full well that if Karen's unintentional fraud was discovered, her entire college journalism career might be ruined. And he would be responsible.

Karen had discovered the deception and was even more furious and chagrined at the deception. But with the unasked-for help of Frankie Baker and Josh Ferguson, who discreetly "withdrew" her article from the competition, the potential disaster had been averted.

As a result, Daniel and his friends were distinctly *persona non grata* with Karen and her whole crowd. It didn't come as any real surprise to him that the doors of *The Red and the Gold* had been slammed in his face.

Roxanne has been studying Daniel's dark face, trying to come up with the right tactic for talking him out of his distressing attitude toward the current Kennedy regime. "Well," she began defensively, "if they'd played fair with you, you'd be an editor on the paper now. But they didn't, and that's why I think you should run against — "

"If *I'd* played fair with *them*, they might've played fair with me," Daniel interrupted in a matter-of-fact tone.

Rox glanced around her at the surrounding tables, then lowered her voice so only Daniel could hear her. "Are you trying to say you're sorry you put Lily up to that interview for the paper?" she accused him in a sharp whisper.

Daniel shrugged. "Maybe I am," he whispered back. "Maybe I'm sorry I used Lily that way. And Karen Davis, too. She never did anything to hurt me."

Roxanne shook her head in disbelief. She adjusted the straps of her tank top impatiently. She had better talk some sense back into Daniel, and fast. "I can't believe you're going soft on that Kennedy crowd," she declared, raising her voice to a normal pitch. "That fake interview was no more than they deserved. It would have served Karen right if that article had won the contest and she got completely nailed. . . ."

Daniel silenced Roxanne with a loud "Ssh." Lily was heading in their direction with her lunch tray, weaving among the tables and smiling at friends along the way. Lily had knowingly made up the interview for Karen and Brian; she'd tapped the best of her acting ability to play the part of a former runaway now making good at a suburban high school. But although she'd done the interview for the paper and on the air at WKND, she was never told how far the prank had gone. Daniel, Rox, and the others knew if kind-hearted Lily had found out about the contest she would have stopped Karen from submitting the article, so they'd kept the truth from her. Lily felt lousy *enough* about the interview — she later confessed to them that she wished she'd never done it — "exercise in acting" or not. There didn't seem to be any reason to let her in on the contest scandal now. It was one secret Lily should never find out about. "Let's change the subject," Daniel hissed.

Lily slid her tray onto the table next to Daniel. Her black T-shirt dress and black tights made her fair skin look even fairer, but the fun-loving expression in her eyes gave her an all-over glow. "Hi, gang!" she said brightly.

Daniel's scowl melted into a smile. "Hey, Lil," he responded with genuine affection.

Even Roxanne unbent a little, although there wasn't much love lost between the two girls. "What *are* you eating, Lily?" she asked with a grimace.

Lily stared down at her tray. "Peanut butter and grape jelly on white with a side of fries. Yummy, huh?"

Zachary grinned. "She's carb-loading, like I do during football season. You need your strength for rehearsals, right, Lil?"

"Right." Lily tore the crust off her sandwich and took a large bite. She chewed appreciatively. "As good as expected," she announced.

Roxanne poked without much interest at her own lunch. "Well, Lily, you arrived just in time," she informed the other girl. "We wouldn't want to make a decision as big as this without you!"

"As big as what?" Lily's blue eyes widened with curiosity. She glanced from Rox to Daniel to Zack and back to Rox again.

Roxanne turned to Daniel, but he only shrugged, so she answered Lily's question herself. "As big as deciding that Daniel should run for student body president! He hasn't actually said he would yet," she conceded, "but I'm wearing him down."

"I bet you are," Lily observed with a giggle. Daniel looked away.

"It's not a laughing matter," Rox chastised. "He *has* to run. It's his moral obligation! We ex-Stevenson students deserve full representation at this school. We're being denied our rights."

Lily tipped her head to the side. "Do you really think that's true, Rox?" she wondered. "I mean, maybe you *do* think it's true, but that hasn't been the case for me. I didn't have any problem getting on the forensics team right off the bat, or getting cast in *The Fantasticks*."

"That's because the wimpy drama kids control that stuff," Rox insisted. "Everything controlled by 'the crowd,' which is just about everything else, is what we're being excluded from. The crowd hates everyone from Stevenson!"

"What about Frankie?" Zachary asked innocently.

Roxanne swiveled in her chair. Sure enough, there was Frances Baker, securely ensconced at the crowd's table with her insipid, hick boyfriend. Frankie was a real sore point with Rox these days. The two girls had been best friends for years.

Pale, shy, intellectual Frankie had always been completely overshadowed by the bewitching, super-outgoing Roxanne. A radical change had come over Frankie not long after they transferred from Stevenson, though. Her old dependence on Roxanne for a social life and self-esteem had gradually dissolved. Now she was wearing make-up, styling her hair differently. Wost of all, she was dating a Kennedy boy — even if he wasn't much to look at, Roxanne thought — and occupying the place at the Kennedy "in" table that she, Roxanne, should have.

After the stunt Frankie and her boyfriend had pulled, stealing Karen's article from the contest headquarters at Georgetown so the editor of *The Red and the Gold* wouldn't be disqualified, Roxanne had declared that she would never forgive her. Frankie clearly didn't feel any loyalty toward her old Stevenson friends, so there was no reason they should be loyal to her.

Roxanne snorted. "The only reason the crowd let Frankie in is because she probably does all their math homework," she said cuttingly.

Zachary laughed in spite of himself. "That's a good deal!" He himself had been benefiting from Frankie's brilliance since she became his math tutor.

Rox treated him to a withering stare. "This isn't a joke, Zack."

He adopted a look of mock seriousness. "Sorry, Rox."

Lily craned her slender neck, scanning the cafeteria for signs of this ominous, monstrous "crowd." She didn't see any group that looked half as dangerous as the one Rozanne described. "Who exactly is in 'the crowd'?" she asked, still looking for Karen, whom she remembered from the interview, and Frankie, apparently the crowd's newest inductee.

"You know: Greg, Jeremy, Holly. . . ." Roxanne began rattling off the names, counting them on her fingers.

Lily wrinkled her nose. "Not their names, their faces." She'd spent most of her time since she transferred at the Little Theater, and while she'd made some new friends in the drama crowd, she hadn't been paying much attention to the Kennedy social scene at large. And after that stupid article about her in the paper, Lily had done her best to stay out of sight. She couldn't have picked out Greg or Jeremy or Holly from among the cafeteria's occupants if her life depended on it.

Roxanne pointed with one coral-colored fingernail. "There," she said.

Lily looked to where Roxanne was pointing. At a large round table in the corner she saw Frankie and her new boyfriend, and Karen and *her* boyfriend Brian from the radio station. And more people that she didn't recognize, and — Lily's heart leaped and then fell. Sitting between two strangers was the boy she'd been looking for all week, ever since she'd met him in the costume room at the Little Theater. *Jonathan.*

Lily's mouth went dry from the simultaneous thrill of seeing him and the ache of disappointment. "That's . . . that's the crowd?" she said, her usually expressive voice flat.

"That's them," Rox affirmed.

"That boy . . . Jonathan, I think? The one with the blue oxford shirt. Is he part of the crowd?" Lily hoped against hope she'd say no, but Roxanne's next words were crushing.

"*Part* of the crowd? He *is* the crowd!" Roxanne scowled, remembering her thwarted scheme to use Jonathan as a stepping stone in her climb right to the top of the Kennedy power structure. "He's the student activities director. If the crowd runs Kennedy, he runs the crowd."

Lily couldn't quite believe it. "Are they really all that bad?" she asked. "They don't *look* any different from any other Kennedy kids. Except maybe cuter," she added, her eyes glued to Jonathan's handsome, animated face.

"Cute, my foot!" Rox sniffed. "They're all the ultimate snobs. You remember how they treated Daniel at the newspaper? Well, that's just one example of the way they do things and the way they deal with anyone who's not one of them."

"Oh," Lily said out loud. Inside, she thought dismally, Oh, Jonathan. Her heartbeat had slowed, and now she would have sworn she could feel it break just a little. She'd found Jonathan only to discover that he belonged to the crowd that hated everyone from Stevenson. The boy whose gray eyes had sent stars flying into her own had turned out to be Public Enemy Number One!

Chapter 4

"Good morning, folks. Or is it good afternoon? Good lunchtime? Well, whatever!" Josh Ferguson ran a hand through his jet-black hair, then adjusted the microphone. "Brian Pierson'll be on in a few minutes with the latest discs, but first I'm going to let you in on what's happening at Kennedy," he continued. "I wouldn't want you to be the last to know!"

Josh was a junior being groomed to take over WKND, the Kennedy High radio station, when Brian graduated. He and his new show, *Cloaks and Jokes*, had become an instant hit. Josh considered storytelling his forte, but with all the airtime Brian had been giving him lately he was learning more and more about music and newscasting.

Now Josh shuffled his color-coded index cards. "The race for student body president is heating up," he informed the WKND audience.

"Now, in addition to previously announced candidates Laura Hoch, Michelle Linwood, Greg Montgomery, and Seth Weinstein; Daniel Tackett, the former editor of *The Stevenson Sentinel*, has entered the running. There's a lot of talent there, and I think Kennedy can consider itself lucky at the prospect of having any one of those five students serve as president next year. The candidates are presently gearing up for the convention in ten days, so stay tuned."

Josh took a deep breath and looked up, about to plunge into the next topic. Through the glass-paned wall of the soundproof broadcasting booth, he could see the door to the outer office swing open. A tall slim girl with pale ash-blonde hair closed the door carefully behind her. When she met his eyes through the window, her delicate features blossomed into a smile. Josh grinned back. No matter what his mood, good or bad, Frankie could make it better just by smiling or holding his hand. They hadn't been going out for very long, but already Josh was starting to wonder how he ever got along without her. She was the best friend anyone could ever have.

"Another date you've probably already put on your calendar, if you're as corny as I am, is the junior-senior prom, which will be two weeks from Friday," Josh continued conversationally. "Tickets are on sale now in the cafeteria. If you buy 'em early, you can get one of the balloons that'll decorate the gym printed with your name and your date's. A pretty great souvenir the two of you can fight over at the end of the evening! Don't forget, though, a date isn't a must for the prom. *All* juniors and seniors are welcome! And as the soda-fountain girl in Raspberry Patch could tell you" — Josh winked at Frankie as he referred to a character in the fictional town that was the subject of many on-air anecdotes, a character inspired by his first encounter with her — "love and happiness can be waiting for you where you least expect them, anywhere, anytime."

He pushed his horn-rimmed glasses up on his nose and then tried not to laugh into the mike as Frankie blew him an exaggerated kiss. "Finally, tomorrow is opening night for the spring musical, *The Fantasticks*. It's running this weekend and next, and if you don't go see it, you're really missing something." The door to the office bounced open again, and Brian Pierson breezed in. He had a brand-new record in his hand, which he waved at Josh through the window pane. "Uh-oh," Josh warned his listeners, "the boss has just arrived, and he's got some new vinyl in his hand. No telling how bizarre, though. I'll leave you with a more down-to-earth sound. Talk to you tomorrow!" Josh cut in a record he had cued up. A few seconds later the WKND audience was listening to Lone Justice, a rock-country band Josh liked. He slipped out of the booth as Brian stepped in, slapping his friend on the back as he passed.

As soon as the door clicked shut behind Brian, Josh grabbed Frankie around the waist and twirled her through the office, half-tripping over a stack of records that needed re-filing. Frankie giggled self-consciously. "Josh, aren't you supposed to be helping Brian? This isn't very dignified behavior for the heir apparent to WKND!"

Josh kissed her nose. "You want me to put you down? But we're sharing a romantic moment!"

"True. Your glasses are already getting steamed up!" Frankie teased him with a smile.

With an "oomph," Josh dropped her back on her feet. "Can't have that," he acknowledged, removing his glasses to wipe the lenses. "At least not in the main office." He gave Frankie a bold wink. "There's always the record closet, though."

Frankie laughed. More than once she and Josh had interrupted Karen and Brian sneaking a kiss while they were supposedly filing albums. "I'll pass," she said, a little regretfully. "I only have a second anyway."

"That's right, don't you have a tutoring date?" Josh had wrapped an arm fondly around Frankie's shoulders. They strolled together to the desk in the far corner of the office, where they could snuggle out of sight of Brian and the broadcasting booth window.

Frankie looked at her watch with a sigh. "Yeah, I do, in a couple of minutes." She tutored Zachary McGraw, a fellow ex-Stevenson classmate, in math. Zack had bought computer-whiz Frankie's tutoring services at a recent prom fundraiser. Students had donated their time and belongings to be auctioned off to the highest bidder, with the proceeds going toward paying for the prom. The money was primarily to cover the booking of a very hot, but also very expensive,

D.C. band. Frankie's four-session tutoring offer should have expired before now, only Zack had postponed their last meeting because of track.

Josh blinked appealingly at Frankie through his now fog-free glasses. "Can't you skip it and stay here with me? Old what's-his-name won't mind."

Frankie laughed. "Zack probably wouldn't mind, but we might as well get this last session over with. Then I'll have all my lunch periods and afternoons free to hang out with you!"

"I guess you're right." Josh sighed heavily, pretending to be deeply disappointed. Then he brightened. "I guess a few minutes of the beautiful soda-fountain girl's time is better than none!"

Frankie's cheeks grew warm with a blush. She wasn't sure if she'd ever get entirely used to Josh's loving admiration of her. Not that she didn't enjoy it. She was as crazy about him as he was about her. But for such a long time — all her life, actually — Frankie had thought of herself as a plain Jane. She'd always excelled academically, but never flaunted her gifts and abilities. People always described her as quiet and shy, and she shared their opinion. No one had made Frankie feel like that more than Rox Easton, who'd been her closest, and practically only, friend for so many years. Sometimes Frankie could hardly believe she'd put up with Rox's bullying and manipulation for so long. They'd had many fun times together, it was true. But the reality was that before, securely under Roxanne's wing and in her shadow, Frankie had been an invisible person, inside and out. Since she'd broken away from Rox's influence, and since she and Josh had fallen in love, Frankie felt more attractive, more interesting, more confident, and more independent than ever before in her life.

The transformation hadn't happened overnight, though. When they'd first transferred from Stevenson this past January, Frankie let Roxanne talk her into fixing the computerized Valentine match-up so Rox would have dates with four different guys. When Rox then failed to become a member of the popular crowd, she tried to drag Frankie along with her on her anti-Kennedy crusade. But soon Frankie realized that all her own contacts with the crowd had been very positive. Jonathan, Katie, Greg, Diana — they couldn't have been nicer to her. The more time she spent with them, and she was spending a lot now that she was dating Josh, the more she liked them. She was finding out what real friends were like.

Now she snuggled under Josh's arm, tipping her face up to his. "The soda-fountain girl's happiest moments are the ones she spends with you," she said with a smile.

"That's exactly the way it should be," Josh declared. They were just about to kiss when a loud knock on the door caused them to spring apart. Josh let go of Frankie so fast she almost fell off the desk. A student Frankie recognized from Stevenson stuck his head into the office.

"Mind if I hang a campaign poster on the door?" the boy asked.

Josh shrugged. "Sure, why not." He noticed the boy's T-shirt, which read STEVENSON HIGH

SCHOOL WRESTLING. "By the way, who's the poster for?" he asked.

He and Frankie both knew what the answer would be before he gave it. "Daniel Tackett."

The door clicked shut, and Frankie and Josh exchanged a glance. "Surprise, surprise," she said, shaking her head in amazement.

"I really can't believe how fast Daniel has moved!" Josh said. "He only declared his candidacy two days ago, and already Kennedy is wallpapered with his face!"

Frankie opened the office door and studied the poster taped on it. "*And* his name," she added. The poster was eye-catching and attractive . . . and definitely a professional product. At the top in bold, royal blue letters it said RADICAL. At the bottom, in slightly smaller letters, it read: DANIEL TACKETT. A CHANGE FOR THE BETTER. In the middle, a big black-and-white picture of Daniel confronted the viewer with a direct, no-nonsense stare. The photographer had captured Daniel's best qualities, Frankie thought. His expression was intense, unshirking. There was no hint that the honesty and integrity his eyes promised could be very selective. Sure, Daniel was honest, even painfully so — when it suited him. But Frankie knew as well as anybody how deceptive he could be. It had been Daniel's idea to set Karen up to do the false interview; he'd masterminded the entire scheme. A half-smile touched Frankie's lips. She supposed she should feel one percent grateful to Daniel for his treachery. After all, if it weren't for him, Karen would never have entered her article in the contest, thus paving the way for

Frankie and Josh to heroically steal it right out of the contest headquarters at the Georgetown journalism department and then, in the aftermath of their adventure, fall into each other's arms for a sweet, first kiss.

As Frankie pushed the WKND door shut, she saw two students walk by sporting showy DANIEL TACKETT FOR PRESIDENT buttons. She shook her head again. "It's really incredible," she said to Josh. "I mean, two days ago no one knew who Daniel was! At least, nobody but the Stevenson kids. Now he's practically as well known as the *real* President."

Josh nodded. "I know. I really didn't need to announce on the radio today that he's running. With all those posters he's been putting up, it's not exactly news."

"What do you think his chances are?" Frankie asked curiously.

Now Josh opened the outer door to examine the poster himself. "Well, you know what I think of him personally. He's not going to buy *my* vote with this stuff. But in general?" Josh paused a moment. "I'd say he's a serious contender. He may even give Greg a run for his money."

Josh closed the door and headed to the record closet. Frankie lifted an armload of albums and followed him in. A moment later they were both busy filing.

"G is for Grateful Dead and Peter Gabriel," Frankie chanted as she slipped the records into their places. "Led Zeppelin, Suzanne Vega, Bruce Springsteen, Bruce Springsteen, Bruce Springsteen. . . ."

"The Boss is still big at WKND. The legacy of Peter Lacey," Josh explained, referring to the recent Kennedy graduate who'd managed the radio station before Brian.

Frankie paused in her filing, still holding up a copy of *Born in the U.S.A*. "What do you think would happen if a former Stevenson student was elected student body president at Kennedy?" she asked suddenly. "Do you think it *would* make 'a change for the better'?"

Josh wrinkled his forehead. "Maybe. If that's what the person really wanted to achieve. If he or she didn't only want to be president because of sour grapes."

Frankie was thoughtfully silent for a moment. Then she observed, "Either way, Daniel's campaign has 'Roxanne' written all over it. She's certainly thorough! She'd run for president herself if she thought anyone would vote for her. Instead, I'll bet she put Daniel up to running. He's got more of a chance. She'll just be the power behind the throne."

"His secretary of state," Josh suggested.

"His chief of staff," Frankie quipped.

"Well, he may be a contender," Josh predicted, "but Greg should still pull it off." He crawled out of the closet and then back in again with another stack of records.

Frankie thought of Greg's modest, photocopied posters hanging alongside Daniel's huge, glossy advertisements. Greg might be the better candidate, but it seemed more than possible that a lot of Kennedy students could simply be brainwashed into believing otherwise. "I hope so," was all she said aloud. She had been staring absently at the Bruce Springsteen album she was holding, and now she refocused on Josh. He was looking at her strangely. "What?" she asked, self-consciously adjusting her new headband, which swept back her hair.

Josh smiled sheepishly. "I was just thinking about the day we met. It was right here, remember?"

"Sure I remember," Frankie said softly. "I'll admit I didn't know it then, but that was the best day of my life!"

Josh bent forward to give Frankie a hug and then sat back to smile at her. "We have a lot to look forward to, don't we? The prom. . . ."

Frankie's eyes sparkled. "I can't wait!"

They were leaning toward each other across a stack of records when a noise in the outer office caused them both to jump back. *Born in the U.S.A.* flew out of Frankie's hands and hit the wall with a clunk. "Oops!" she exclaimed with a giggle.

This time it was Zachary McGraw who interrupted them. He peeked around the door of the record closet, a strand of blond hair falling into his eyes. "Here you are, Frankie!" he said, his voice warm and friendly.

Zack grinned and Frankie grinned back. Neither saw the shocked expression that crossed Josh's face. "Hey, Zack! Oops, am I late for our tutoring session?"

Zack waved a hand. Under the short sleeves of his Ohio State T-shirt, his arm muscles rippled impressively. "Naw. I was waiting for you in my algebra room since that's where we met before, but then someone suggested looking for you here. It's no problem." He looked from Frankie to Josh, as if noticing the other boy's presence for the first time. "Are you guys in the middle of something? Should I come back later?"

Josh snorted. Frankie restrained an embarrassed giggle.

"No, we're not in the middle of anything. We really should get started with your math. If you want to wait outside, I'll be right out."

"Sure thing." Frankie watched Zack amble obediently toward the door. She hadn't seen much of him since she and Josh got together. And amazingly, she'd thought about him even less. She was secretly astonished that she could have forgotten him so totally. It wasn't that long ago that Zachary, a long-time friend from Stevenson, was her primary preoccupation. But as soon as she fell for Josh, her old crush on Zack had faded into dust. It was funny how those things happened.

Frankie looked over to find Josh watching her, his eyes wide. "*That's* your tutoring student?" he asked in an odd voice.

"Yeah — you'll get to know his name real well next football season." Frankie got to her feet and started collecting her books. "I really should go."

"I was expecting some dopey-looking nerd," Josh admitted. "Not Rocky Junior."

Frankie laughed at his jealous frown. "You're crazy," she said affectionately. "And besides, jocks are people, too!" Josh's frown melted into a grin. "I'll see you after school." Frankie gave him a quick kiss and headed for the door.

Once they were in the hallway heading for the school's north wing and Zack's algebra room, he offered to carry Frankie's books. As she handed them over, she thought it was fitting that today should be her last time tutoring him. A chapter in her life had been closed — her friendship with Roxanne, her infatuation with Zachary, all her old insecurities were part of her past. As for the chapters ahead, they promised to be bright, mostly because her very first boyfriend had turned out to be the most wonderful boy in the world.

Chapter 5

Lily opened her eyes as wide as she could, raising her eyebrows up so high they nearly disappeared into her short blonde hair. Then she smiled as wide as she could, first with her lips pressed tightly together and then with them parted and as many teeth showing as possible. Finally she wiggled her ears and then tipped her head back, rolling it loosely around on her shoulders in an attempt to relax.

The lights above the dressing table bathed her and the other girls in an eerie glow. The clock near the door of the changing room registered the passing minutes with loud, ominous ticks. In another fifteen minutes, a bell would ring signaling five minutes until curtain. It was the opening night of *The Fantasticks*.

Lily took a deep breath, inhaling all the way down to her toes. She was so nervous and excited she was shaking a little. Not that performing was anything new to her. She'd participated in lots of dramatic and musical productions at Stevenson. Only a couple of months ago she'd also gone in front of a large audience and a panel of judges to win the humorous improvisation contest for Kennedy at the University of Virginia Invitational Forensics Tournament. Still, every time she went onstage was like the first time. The thrill was always there. It was what Lily wanted to do for the rest of her life — be onstage, as a stand-up comedian.

Now Lily darted a glance at the girl sitting next to her, Kathleen Ransom, a senior. If she was tingling with anxious anticipation, imagine what Kathleen, the lead, was feeling! For a moment, Lily envied Kathleen. There was something undeniably glamorous about playing the lead. But she loved her own role. She'd had and would have plenty of opportunities to play the "girl" in the standard "boy meets girl" stories; the mime role was more expressionistic, a real creative challenge. It was a role she could make entirely her own through the movements of her face, hands, and body, sparking the audience's imagination in a way that no speaking character ever could.

Lily looked at the clock and realized she'd better get moving with her makeup. The makeup for the part of the mime was a lot more extensive than the usual pancake, blush, and mascara. First she had to apply whiteface all over, then paint on winglike black eyebrows and line her eyes in a star-shaped pattern. Finally, she'd add a red clown's mouth. When she finished, she would be unrecognizable.

Lily had just dabbed a chalk-white stripe across her face when she felt a tap on her shoulder. It was Marsha Terry, the stage manager, holding a single long-stemmed red rose wrapped in frothy tissue paper.

"For me?" Lily mouthed silently, pointing to herself with an exaggerated look of astonishment.

Marsha laughed. "Yeah, for you. Some guy gave it to me backstage. He asked me to be sure to deliver it to you personally."

Lily took the rose from Marsha, breathed in its fragrance, and then with a great fluttering of her hands she pulled the card from the tiny envelope taped to the paper. But when Lily saw the name on the card, she dropped her mime act. Her jaw fell. The rose was from Jonathan. *Jonathan!* She clasped the card to her chest and then sank back in her chair to read it properly. *Dear Lily,* it began. The handwriting was eccentric, distinguished. Lily's heart galloped. *Dear Lily, I'll be watching tonight — I know you will be 'Fantastick'! Best wishes, Jonathan.*

Suddenly breathless, Lily dropped the card on the dressing table next to the bouquet of spring flowers her family had sent. Jonathan was going to be in the audience tonight. He'd come to see her! Just like he said he would the day they'd talked in the costume storeroom. She hadn't dared to believe he really would.

Lily felt like singing, but she didn't want to fall out of character. So instead, she sang silently to herself as she finished making up. Jonathan Preston was in the audience in the theater, she thought. It had to mean he liked her as much as she liked him, didn't it?

Lily did a few more minutes of facial warm-ups before the bell rang. Only five minutes until curtain! She grabbed her hat — a straw one with a broad black band and a big yellow daisy — and placed it carefully on her head. As she tipped it over one ear, she thought back to her encounter with Jonathan among the costumes. After his initial huffiness over his fedora, he *had* been friendly and sincerely warm. But then she recalled the recent conversation at the Stevenson lunch table: All Jonathan's friends, and presumably Jonathan himself, hated everyone from Stevenson. Which story was true?

Lily weighed the evidence for a moment. It was clear what Roxanne Easton would say. But Lily had always been one to make up her own mind about people and things, and she thought she had the answer. And Roxanne could be such a loudmouth. What's important, she decided, touching the soft petals of the rose and picking up the card from Jonathan, is that he's here, to see me. He kept his promise. He thinks I'm fantastic! On a whim, she tucked the little card into the front pocket of her baggy gray trousers. It would remind her all through the show that, feud or no feud, maybe there was hope for her and Jonathan after all.

As Lily dashed from the dressing room to join the other members of the cast backstage, she found herself wishing she was wearing Jonathan's fedora instead of her old straw hat. Well, she could pretend she was. After all, that was what acting was all about.

By the time the old green curtain closed with a jerk in front of the cast's final bows, Jonathan's hands stung from clapping so hard. "Bravo!" he yelled, his voice lost in the hubbub of the exiting crowd.

The first performance of *The Fantasticks* had been a tremendous success. The full house had laughed at all the right places and only once had an actor forgotten his lines. Now that the show was over, though, Jonathan had to admit that he couldn't remember much about the plot. Most everything was already a blur except the times when Lily had been onstage. She looked so slender and delicate, but with the slightest movement she could draw all eyes to her and keep them there. She was immensely talented, and Jonathan thought she had stolen the show . . . and his heart.

"Ahem. Ready to go?" Jonathan jumped, suddenly realizing he was the last person in the theater clapping. He turned to see that his "dates" for the evening, Eric and Molly, were waiting for him patiently. Eric was grinning. "I mean, feel free to clap all night if you want to, but I really don't think you're going to get an encore."

Jonathan bent to pull his rumpled fedora out from under his seat. "Right," he said, patting it back into shape.

"So, what's next on the agenda?" Molly asked, reaching her hands up and stretching her tiny, compact frame to its highest.

"The sub shop?" Eric suggested, rubbing his stomach hungrily.

"Why did I even ask?" Molly wondered with a laugh. "It's tough keeping you guys filled up."

She and Eric made their way out to the aisle and started up toward the door, then discovered that once again Jonathan wasn't following them. "Preston!" Molly called back to him. "Are you coming or not?"

Jonathan stepped into the aisle and paused. "Actually," he began, trying to sound casual, "I thought I'd pop backstage for a couple of minutes. There's, um . . . someone, a couple of people I want to say hi to and congratulate. You guys go ahead."

Molly glanced at Eric, one eyebrow raised. Jonathan waited for the teasing questions to come, but Eric didn't give Molly a chance to ask any. He dragged her toward the door, too hungry to be curious himself. "Well, catch up with us later at the sub shop," he invited.

"See you, Jonathan!" Molly added.

Jonathan waved and then started back down the aisle toward the stage. Everything at the stage end of the theater was noise and bustle. The crew was shifting scenery, waving mops and brooms, and retrieving stray props and costume pieces. Each item had to be put back in its proper place, ready for tomorrow night's show, before they could go home.

No one paid much attention to Jonathan as he wove his way through the backstage clutter, heading in the direction of the dressing rooms. When he reached the girls' dressing room he stopped, suddenly uncertain. First of all, he couldn't exactly barge in there and ask for Lily. He'd have to find someone to go in with the message that he was there to see her. Secondly and more important, he didn't really know whether Lily would even want to see him. He'd bought the rose on impulse, and while he knew how *he* felt about sending it — pretty good — he had no idea how *she* felt about receiving it. Maybe there was already a guy in the picture, Jonathan thought. Another actor even. Maybe somebody as un-arty as he was wouldn't be her type.

Well, nothing ventured, nothing gained, he decided gallantly. He took a deep, determined breath and lifted his hand to knock on the door. Before he could, it flew open and he was almost thrown off his feet by Lily herself, followed by some Stevenson kids who had also stopped by to congratulate her. They wandered off noisily, promising to see her later.

"Jonathan!" she exclaimed, her eyes flickering with a combination of surprise, pleasure, and shyness.

"Lily," Jonathan's grin was eager and at the same time awkward. "I just wanted to stop by and say I thought you were . . . the play was . . . congratulations!"

Lily laughed. Only then did Jonathan notice that she'd only removed part of her makeup. She was still half Lily, and half mysterious mime — and in his opinion, absolutely adorable. "Thanks! I'm glad you liked it." She ducked her head, pretending to study the rubber toes of the oversized basketball sneakers she'd worn for her part. "And I'm glad you came."

"I wouldn't have missed it for the world," Jonathan told her sincerely.

They were silent for a few seconds. Jonathan wondered what to say next. He had to think of something — he wasn't ready to leave just yet. It was Lily who spoke up first, though. "Well," she said, waving behind her at the dressing room. "I'd invite you in but. . . !"

He laughed. "That's okay. And hey, am I interrupting you? You sort of looked like you were on your way somewhere important."

Lily looked puzzled. Then she seemed to remember. She put one hand in her front pocket and the half of her face that wasn't made-up went slightly pink. "Oh, that's right! I was on my way to look for something that fell out of my pocket during the show."

"I could help you," Jonathan offered.

"No, really," Lily assured him, her cheek turning even pinker, "I'll find it later I'm sure. Here, you want to sit down and talk for a few minutes?"

Jonathan did, but he wasn't sure where to sit. The only furnishings in the back hallway were paint buckets and boxes. "There aren't any chairs," he pointed out.

Lily smiled mischievously. "I know where there are a few," she said. "This way!" Jonathan followed her back to the main part of the theater. Lily waved a small hand and giggled. "Take your pick!"

Jonathan grabbed her hand, more than a little surprised at his own boldness, and they ran laughing together down the aisle and into one of the rows.

"Seat F-seven," Lily read as she dropped into it. "Front and center!" They gazed for a moment at the now-empty stage.

"How does it feel to be down here in the audience?" Jonathan asked, turning in his seat to study Lily's sharp but delicate profile.

She tipped her head to one side. "It feels . . . *different*," she responded thoughtfully. "It feels far away." She looked at him with wide, curious eyes. "Is that what it felt like to you during the show?"

"No." Jonathan shook his head firmly. "It didn't seem that way at all. I felt close." His expression grew animated, remembering. "When you were onstage, I almost felt like I was up there with you," he admitted.

Lily nodded as if she understood. "I guess that's the whole point. Of acting, I mean. The audience is supposed to feel like they're part of what's happening onstage. If they don't, then the play's a flop."

"Well, *The Fantasticks* was exactly the opposite. It gets a rave review, from Jonathan Preston at least!"

Lily smiled. "Jonathan Preston." She repeated his name in an experimental voice, seeming to test the way it felt to say it. Jonathan liked the way it sounded when she said it. "Jonathan Preston, do you realize we barely even know each other?"

Jonathan was sitting with his long legs propped

up on the seat in front of him. He removed his fedora and slapped it against his knees. "I know," he agreed with a sheepish smile. "It's funny because I feel like I *do* know you, sort of. I mean, I'd like to know you better. . . ." He stopped, embarrassed. "What I'm trying to say is, would you like to go out some time?"

Jonathan held his breath. Lily hesitated, obviously unsure, and he felt his palms grow damp. She was about to blow him off. He must have come across like an idiot.

But when he chanced a look in her direction, she didn't seem disgusted or even disinterested. The glow in her eyes matched the hopeful light in his own. She was experiencing the same attraction he was, he could tell. When she finally spoke, she didn't say "no," but she didn't say "yes" either. "But what about. . . ." Lily's voice faltered slightly. "What about your friends and all?"

Jonathan was confused. "My friends?" he echoed. "What do *they* have to do with it?" He thought maybe Lily was joking. "They don't have to come along!"

Lily laughed nervously, shrugging her slim shoulders underneath her oversized, checkered jacket. "Well, I'm from Stevenson," she explained. "Your crowd — my crowd — "

Jonathan snorted. "Forget about that!" he said with a dismissive wave of his hand. "I haven't been paying any attention to that crazy feud. To tell you the truth, I don't even know what it's all about anymore! And I don't care."

Lily appeared relieved. "Me, either."

"Besides," Jonathan continued, touching her

shoulder, "my friends are great. They don't hold grudges without a reason. Look at Frankie — everyone treats her like we've known her forever. They're bound to like anyone I like. And I like you," he finished simply.

Now Lily accepted his invitation happily. "In that case, you're on!" she exclaimed with a brilliant smile.

Jonathan could hardly believe his luck. He hadn't been sure he would come up with the nerve to ask Lily out, and if he did he wasn't sure she'd even be interested in him. But he had and she was! He was so excited and so proud of himself and of Lily that he couldn't sit still a minute longer. He jumped to his feet, catching his hat as it bounced off his knees. "So, how about tonight?" he asked eagerly.

Lily burst out laughing. "It's already eleven o'clock," she reminded him. "Anyway, I still have to take off my makeup and my costume. After that, in all honesty, I really just want to go home to bed. I'm beat. And I'm performing again tomorrow, and next weekend, too." She saw the disappointment on Jonathan's face and quickly added, "But after that, I'd love to go out with you. After the show closes. Seriously. Okay?"

"Okay," Jonathan agreed. "How about the night after the show closes?"

Lily giggled. "Maybe. We can talk about it."

We can talk about it, Jonathan thought as he walked Lily back to the dressing room. He imagined calling Lily on the phone, just to talk, looking for her in the halls, sitting with her at lunch. It was going to be . . . *fantastic.*

"Hey." They had said good-bye, and Lily was opening the dressing room door but now Jonathan stopped her, putting a hand on her arm. "You were going to look for something, remember? Something that fell out of your pocket."

Lily pushed the hair back from her forehead, her lips curving. "That's all right, I'd never find it." She gazed at him steadily. "And anyhow, I think I found something better."

As Jonathan strode briskly through the theater and out to the lot where his car was parked, he was pretty sure he knew what Lily meant.

Chapter 6

"Eight point five," the bespectacled judge announced. There was scattered applause and the Carrolton High gymnast left the mats with a pleased smile and a flip of her fluffy blonde ponytail.

Katie gulped, suddenly wishing she were back on crutches, safely watching the competition from the bleachers. Instead, she was to perform next. It was her first time back in action since she broke her leg in January, and this was the first event of the afternoon. The floor exercise — never her strongest area. Well, what I lose here I'll make up later on the beam, she told herself as she had dozens of times before in her career. She only wished she could believe it now.

"Kennedy number three?" Katie snapped to attention. That was her. Everyone was waiting! In a few quick steps she was on the mats, setting herself up in the far corner, facing the judges, her coach, and her teammates, with her back to the bleachers. She could feel everyone staring at her, and it was a spooky sensation. All that attention! She used to love it. She had always been in her element when she was in the spotlight, competing. But that was back when she knew she was one of the best, when she routinely led the Kennedy team to victory with one, maybe two, maybe even three first-place scores in any given event. But today she was nervous, almost scared.

Today, for the first time since Katie could remember, she had to prove something to herself about her gymnastics ability. What made it even worse was that she felt she also had to prove it to her teammates, her competitors, the Kennedy fans, even to her mom and younger brother, Danny, who were in the stands somewhere. She could almost hear the whispers: "That's Katie Crawford. She used to be the best gymnast on the team before she was injured." "Is she going to make a comeback?" "I don't know. . . ." Katie squeezed her eyes tightly shut. *Don't think like that,* she lectured herself sternly. *You can do it. You can!*

Katie began her routine. Arms straight up in the air to strike balance and build momentum. She sprinted right into her first tumbling run: a round-off, back handspring, back flip, back flip with a full twist. Her landing was off. Katie winced. Her right leg didn't exactly hurt, but it was definitely a little shaky. She had to take it easy as she executed a series of slower, more graceful control moves and then dashed into another tumbling run. This one was a little better than the first, but again her landing was wobbly. Katie put everything she had into the rest of her routine, but even as she landed — more steadily this time — she knew she hadn't done well. She might not have done anything so drastic as falling, but that was only because she hadn't taken the sort of risks that led to falls. Because she didn't have her ordinary power for pushing off in between jumps, she was forced to perform more conservative moves than she used to — a single twist where she would have done one-and-a-half or two; four tumbles per run instead of five. No, she hadn't fallen, but the nerve, the daring with which she'd always performed had been completely lacking. For all Katie knew, it might never came back. Her leg, her whole body might never regain its old strength and agility.

As she waited nervously for her score, Katie didn't know whether she felt more like cursing or crying. But when her score was called out — a measly 7.0 — she knew. It was all she could do to keep her eyes from filling with tears. Coach Muldoon's reassuring arm around her shoulders only made it harder. A *seven*! Katie had never in her life received such a low score after a relatively clean round. Had she been that bad? It was sure to be one of the lowest scores on the team!

She glanced up at the bleachers as she walked back over to her teammates. There was the usual polite applause for her score. People will clap for anything, she thought grimly, just to be nice. I could have stood in the middle of the mat on my head and they'd still clap automatically! But there was no enthusiasm from the audience like there had been a few minutes before for the girl from

Carrolton. Then Katie realized that wasn't quite true. Two people had actually stood up to applaud. One of course was her mother, she observed with the usual combination of affection and mortification. The other was. . . .

Katie's weak right leg suddenly felt weaker. The other person now resuming his seat was Greg. *Greg*, Katie thought dully. He looked as if he were trying to catch her eye, but she couldn't bear for him to see the tears in her eyes. She looked away from the bleachers, taking a seat on a folding chair along the gym wall. One of her teammates handed her a fluffy white towel, and on the pretext of wiping the sweat from her forehead, Katie dabbed at her eyes. Greg was here. He'd seen her perform. It didn't occur to her to feel glad that he'd come; she was too preoccupied with the fact that he'd witnessed her failure, her 7.0 score. Greg, whose crew team was on its way to being the regional champions, who was running for student body president and would probably win hands-down. Instead of making her feel better, Greg's presence only made Katie feel smaller and more defeated.

She turned her head slightly so she could see Greg out of the corner of her eye. She was just a little bit curious. Who was he with? What was he wearing? It looked like he'd gotten a haircut. Then her attention was drawn away from the bleachers to the door that led from the girls' locker room into the gym. Bolting through it and taking her warm-up pants off as she went was Stacy Morrison.

Katie looked at her watch, flabbergasted. She

had been so anxious about her own performance that she hadn't even noticed Stacy was missing during team warm-ups. She shook her head. The meet had started half an hour ago and Stacy was only showing up now? It was really amazing. Katie couldn't believe anyone could be such a flake. She wondered if Stacy had been goofing off somewhere, or if she just forgot, not sure which would be worse.

Either way, Stacy was here now and it looked as though she'd made it in time to participate. Katie watched as Ms. Muldoon said a few firm, motherly words to her. Stacy listened absently, her hands raised to braid her light brown hair. Only five minutes later, before she'd even had a chance to warm up, Stacy was called for her floor exercise, the last gymnast to perform in that event.

Katie's muscles twinged. Stacy was sure going to be sore tomorrow, but she deserved it. Loosening up with a thorough, all-over warm-up before every practice or meet was a cardinal rule in gymnastics, and every other sport. But Stacy didn't seem to be fazed in the least. Tossing her jacket onto the empty chair next to Katie, she strode casually to the mats. With a smile at the stands where a group of her classmates were laughing and waving, she launched into her routine.

It looked as though Stacy was going to pull it off. Unfortunately, Katie thought resentfully. The younger girl had a rough-edged sort of presence, an eye-catching sparkle. She was naturally fearless, the way Katie had always been, and she attempted more challenging moves than nearly any other girl on the team. But with no warm-up and her usual lack of concentration, what should have been an outstanding routine was sloppy and imprecise. For every clean jump, there was a messy one, or a crooked landing, a half stumble. When it was over, Stacy greeted her 7.5 — higher than her own hard-earned score, Katie thought bitterly — with a careless shrug.

Stacy stopped near Katie to retrieve her jacket. She was about to walk away when the older girl stopped her. "Stacy," Katie said sharply. She knew she probably shouldn't say anything, but she couldn't stop herself. She had always been upfront with her opinions, and she had a pretty definite opinion of Stacy's poor showing in the floor exercise. Suddenly, Katie had to let her feelings all out.

Stacy, chalking her hands, turned back to face Katie with a distracted, friendly smile. "Hmm?"

"Did it ever occur to you that you're wasting your talent?" Katie began in a cold, unbending tone. "That if you keep on approaching your sport like this you might as well not even bother?"

Stacy's smile faded and her hazel eyes widened. This was clearly not what she'd guessed her teammate wanted to say to her. Before she could say anything in protest or self-defense, Katie charged on. "You have a lot of talent, and you should do yourself and everyone else a favor and make the most of it. Then maybe you'd help the team instead of holding it back!"

Now Stacy was too stunned to speak. The two girls stared at one another for a few long moments. As soon as Katie figured her words had had time to sink in, she spun on her heel and marched off to the uneven bars, her next event.

The rest of the meet was uneventful, for Katie at least. Neither she nor Stacy placed in any of the events, although it did look to her as if Stacy, now properly warmed up, put a little more of herself, both body and spirit, into her remaining routines. Katie herself felt relatively strong on the balance beam, which had always been her favorite event. She was still far from one hundred percent, but her 8.0 score was her best of the day.

By the time the last event was over, Katie was starting to feel badly that she'd yelled at Stacy. She'd been unkind and out of line — her remarks hadn't exactly represented constructive criticism. Katie had never really liked Stacy — she was too undisciplined and flighty — but she didn't have to be *mean* to her. After all, they were teammates, and they still had to work out together for the rest of the season. Katie decided she'd find her teammate and apologize before she left the gym.

In the meantime, she scanned the bleachers, which home and visiting fans were quickly leaving. When Greg's faded hunter green polo shirt was nowhere to be seen, she felt a stab of disappointment. He'd left. Katie realized she'd been half-hoping and half-expecting he'd come looking for her after the meet. Now she decided she shouldn't be surprised. It must have been clear to him, even from where he was sitting, that she no longer had what it took to be a winner. What could he possibly have to say to her? What did they have in common anymore?

Katie hung her head glumly, hiding her eyes behind the curtain of her auburn bangs. She remembered she'd meant to talk to Stacy just as Stacy herself called out to her.

"Katie . . ." Stacy began hesitantly.

"Oh, Stacy," Katie said, coming back to earth with a start. She paused a moment to get her courage up. "I'm glad you're still here. I wanted to tell you I'm sorry. For losing my temper, I mean. I had no right to do that." She forced a smile, but it didn't quite reach her eyes. "I guess I've just been upset about other things. About my own performance and about . . . well, other things. I shouldn't have taken it out on you. Forgive me?"

Stacy shook her head emphatically. Her hair, now loose, swung forward over one red-and-gold leotarded shoulder. "But Katie, what I wanted to tell *you* is that I realized you were right. Everything you said about me is true. I mean, it's what Ms. Muldoon has been saying to me all along." She laughed wryly. "I just never really thought about it until I heard it from you." Then Stacy's expression became almost shy. "You'd probably never believe it to look at me, Katie," she added in a confiding tone, "but . . . I've been looking up to you ever since I tried out for the team this winter."

"Me?" Katie's laugh was rueful, but inside she was flattered. "I wasn't much to look up to today."

"But you were," Stacy insisted. "I wish I was more like you. I love gymnastics, I really do," she said sincerely. "I'd like to get better. I'd like to be as good as you were. *Are*. I just have to learn how to be more disciplined."

Katie studied Stacy's fresh, eager face. Suddenly she felt a little of her own energy returning. Maybe Stacy wasn't so bad after all. She was definitely young and immature, but Stacy was also a challenge. And Katie'd always liked challenges. "I'll tell you what," she offered after thinking for a moment. "If you want, I'll stay at the gym a while longer this afternoon and give you a few pointers. Okay?"

Stacy's face fell slightly and Katie could sense her balking. "Well, to tell you the truth, I was planning to go out for pizza with a bunch of my friends." Stacy pointed toward the door at some sophomores who were waiting for her. "Maybe some other — "

Katie interrupted her. It was time for the first lesson. If Stacy really wanted to improve, she'd listen. "The extra workout is more important," she told her firmly. "Say no to your friends, this once."

Stacy held Katie's eyes, her internal struggle visible. Finally she nodded. "All right," she agreed, looking sobered by Katie's strength. "I will!" Then she smiled playfully. "This *once*."

Katie grinned back. "This once."

Stacy trotted over to her friends to give them the news and then rejoined Katie on the mats. "So, where do we start?" she asked eagerly.

"At the beginning, I guess," Katie answered, hoping they wouldn't be bothered by the people still milling around the gym. As they started working out, it struck her that Stacy wasn't the only person starting over. In their own separate ways, a new beginning was something they both needed.

Chapter 7

"Yee-ha!" Bob Murphy popped the cork off a bottle of "champagne" that was really carbonated grape juice. Lily threw her mime's hat up in the air and then shrieked as Bob pointed the foaming bottle at her.

Joyful chaos reigned backstage at the Little Theater. The final performance of *The Fantasticks* had been as exhilarating as opening night. The arts page of *The Red and the Gold* had praised it as one of the best productions Kennedy had ever attempted. Now, though, it was hard to believe that after all those hours of rehearsal the show was over. It was a relief, but the last performance was also a little sad. The cast had grown close, and with no more drama productions scheduled for the rest of the school year, they wouldn't be seeing as much of each other. They decided to spend the rest of this last evening together by throwing a celebratory cast and crew party at Kathleen's house.

Lily volunteered to pick up some food on her way over. After changing quickly into her jeans and tie-dyed T-shirt, she hopped into her rattly Chevy pickup and roared into town, heading for the sub shop. She was as sad as anyone that the play was over, but at the same time she'd been looking forward to this night for more than a week. Now that she didn't have *The Fantasticks* to keep her busy, she could go on a date with Jonathan! They'd bumped into each other at school a few times and even talked twice on the phone, and she knew he was looking forward to it as much as she was. Lily still hadn't gotten her nerve up to approach him at his crowd's table in the cafeteria, but that would be easier after they'd gone out once or twice.

She glanced at her reflection in the rearview mirror as she turned onto Main Street, past the Rose Hill Post Office. She hadn't yet removed her makeup; she thought it would be kind of funny to spend a few hours with it still on. Lily could easily remove it once she was at the party. She chuckled to herself as she pulled into the last empty parking space in front of the sub shop. With her white face and elaborately made-up eyes, not to mention the heavy-duty hairspray that made her hair stand up even more than it already did, she didn't look like the average sub shop regular.

As she jammed on the truck's parking brake and then jumped down onto the pavement, Lily decided she would tip the person who waited on her five bucks if he or she took her order with a straight face. No such luck. The guy behind the takeout counter burst out laughing as soon as he saw her standing there.

"I'd like two dozen small Italian subs, a couple dozen bags of potato chips and those cheese doodly things." Lily made the request with a completely straight face.

"What's this, a midnight snack for you and the rest of the circus?" he joked, slicing a loaf of Italian bread in half. "Or has Halloween come early this year?"

"Actually, it's for a costume party at the state prison," Lily informed him blandly.

"Oh." The boy didn't have a comeback for that one. "Well, your subs'll be ready in a few minutes. You can wait over there if you want." He pointed to a row of stools by the front window. Lily took a seat and twirled on the stool, her legs dangling. She'd only been in the sub shop once before, to grab a milk shake with a couple of fellow cast members after a weeknight rehearsal. She knew it was one of the most popular hangouts in town for the kids from Kennedy. It was certainly packed to the rafters right now, she observed. Probably typical for a Saturday night.

She scanned the room curiously. The decor was eclectic to say the least, and unconventional Lily liked it immediately. The walls and ceilings were hung with all sorts of crazy things, ranging from university pennants to an old motorcycle to a genuine moose head. A life-sized wooden Indian manned one murky corner, and old stuffed bear another; an ornate jukebox, presently blasted the Rolling Stones. Wood booths lining the walls surrounded a group of long picnic tables.

Lily jiggled her feet to the beat, humming. She found herself wishing she knew someone there, that *she* was hanging out with friends at the sub shop. Just then she realized that she *did* know someone. She was staring at a wonderfully familiar face — Jonathan! He and his friends were sitting at one of the longest of the long picnic tables, way in the back of the room. Lily's heart somersaulted. Should she go over and say hi? Or should she grab her subs and hightail it back to her truck? Maybe Jonathan wouldn't see her. Maybe he would see her but he wouldn't recognize her. But at that moment Jonathan, who was facing in her direction, did notice her. He looked away, then did a double take. Because of my makeup? Lily wondered. Jonathan had jumped to his feet and was striding toward her, a jubilant smile on his face. *Because of me!* Lily realized, her face flushing underneath the makeup.

Jonathan stopped in front of her, leaning close to peer under her bangs into her eyes. "Is that you, Lily?" he asked, pretending to be unsure.

"Yep!" Lily answered, delighted.

"How'd it go tonight?" Jonathan started to settle onto a stool next to her while she told him about their last performance.

Suddenly, he sprang up. "I'd really like you to meet my friends. Eric and Greg are having a milk-shake-drinking contest — it's shaping up to be a fun night."

"I'm sure!" Lily laughed as she slid off her stool. "All right. I'd like to say hi." She was happy to hear she sounded more carefree and confident than she felt. "But I only have a minute," she warned Jonathan. "A lot of hungry people are waiting for me and my subs."

"No problem!" He grabbed her hand, his touch sending a warm current up her arm, and squeezed her through the crush of sub shop customers. His eagerness made her feel good. Jonathan couldn't be too worried about her being from Stevenson if he was this psyched about presenting her to his friends.

As they approached the table, Lily heard everyone laughing and cheering on the milk-shake-drinking contest. Jonathan pulled her over but the sub shop was so crowded, hardly anyone noticed her. A few of Jonathan's friends smiled at her crazy makeup but, besides that, Lily could have been from outer space and it wouldn't have mattered. The kids at the table were all in their own separate conversations. Some were talking seriously, but most of them were just hanging out and celebrating a big Saturday night. They were just like her Stevenson friends, Lily thought.

Jonathan immediately joined in the joking around. "Oh, no way, Monty! Don't tell me you're wimping out after only four shakes!"

Greg pushed the half-empty paper cup away from him, toward the others he and Eric had already downed. "Off my case," Greg begged, patting his stomach tenderly. "I don't see *you* drinking any!"

"That's because *I'm* not dumb enough to participate in such a lame contest," Jonathan reminded him. He turned to Lily with a grin.

Lily smiled back, and then continued to check out his friends. Several of them looked familiar from the lunch table in the cafeteria that Roxanne had pointed out to her. Lily thought she recognized Frankie when she first walked over, but she must have left the table to place an order or something. At any rate, all of Jonathan's friends seemed nice. He hadn't introduced her yet, but Lily felt comfortable enough around them to want to sit down and get to know these "horrible" crowd members. Unfortunately, she had to get back to the cast party. But maybe Jonathan would bring her back sometime . . . maybe on one of their dates.

Then, suddenly, Lily gasped. Just two feet away from her sat Karen and Brian. They weren't facing Lily, but if they should happen to turn around, Karen and Brian would instantly recognize her. What would happen if they saw her with Jonathan?

Jonathan continued to chatter on, but Lily had to get out of there. Fast. Without a word, she bolted through the crowd for the front door.

"Wait!" Jonathan called, and finally caught up with her. "Is everything all right?"

"Oh, yeah, sure," Lily stammered. "I was having such a good time I completely forgot about the party . . . and the subs. I have to go — I'm sorry I couldn't stay longer with your friends."

Jonathan walked back with her to the counter and insisted on paying for everything. The subs were gigantic and it looked to Lily as if she would have to make two trips. Jonathan wouldn't hear of it. "Let me carry this stuff out to your car for you," he said firmly.

"Truck," Lily corrected with a smile. She had to stop thinking of the near-catastrophe that had just occurred in the sub shop.

"Truck?" he repeated blankly.

"Truck! I drive a truck."

"Of course!" He grinned as he scooped up the grocery bags full of subs. "A girl like you wouldn't drive just an ordinary car like everyone else."

Lily rolled her eyes. "It's nothing special," she assured him, holding the door open. Jonathan stumbled through sideways, the sandwiches nearly spilling out of the bag. "Wait'll you see it."

When Jonathan saw the Chevy he whistled admiringly. "Man, this thing is a relic!" He ran a finger across the rusted-over yellow paint on the hood and gave one of the sturdy front tires a playful kick. "How do you keep it running?"

Lily shrugged and smiled. "Magic, I guess."

"Yes, magic," Jonathan said. His serious look made Lily tingle. She was momentarily tongue-tied, something that didn't happen to her very often. It had been a long time since a guy had had this kind of overwhelming effect on her. It felt kind of nice.

Jonathan had opened the door on the passenger side. Lily knew he didn't have to actually climb into the cab and close the door behind him in order to unload the subs, but he did and she was glad. Now they sat side by side, with the sandwiches at their feet and about a mile of the truck's wide front seat between them.

"Um . . . do you want to go with me to the cast party?" Lily invited on a whim.

Jonathan looked regretful. "Thanks, but I can't. It sounds like fun, but I really shouldn't ditch my friends."

Lily noticed he didn't make any move to leave, however. She wondered how long she could keep him there. "Thanks for helping," she said, looking down at the bags of food. "The cast of *The Fantasticks* is forever in your debt!"

"It was nothing," Jonathan protested modestly. "Just look at it as my contribution to the arts at Kennedy High!"

Lily wrinkled her nose. "That still sounds kind of strange to me," she admitted. She turned to face Jonathan, tucking her feet up on the seat under her. "I mean, hearing myself referred to as being from Kennedy and not Stevenson. I'm getting used to it, though. And I think your friends are really nice. I was impressed."

Jonathan's gray eyes crinkled at the corners. "What can I say — they're a great crew. And they're going to be crazy about you."

"Well . . . we'll see," Lily said quietly.

Jonathan's expression became serious. "No, I meant that." He looked down, pretending to study a tear in the truck's upholstery. "I'm really glad I bumped into you here," he confessed. He looked up again and held her gaze. "It's great to see you."

"I know," Lily agreed. "Our paths don't seem to cross much."

"Yeah, we've got to do something about that." Jonathan shook a finger at her. "And now that your play is over, you don't have any more excuses. You promised you'd go out with me, remember?" He inched a little nearer to her on the seat. "You're cornered!"

Lily wasn't going anywhere. The light in her deep blue eyes was encouraging. "So, we're finally going to do something together. But what?"

Jonathan scratched his head. "I hadn't really thought about that," he admitted, leaning forward to flip on the radio. "I suppose we could do anything. We could . . . um . . . uh. . . ." He looked at Lily for inspiration.

"We could . . . take a bus to Atlantic City and gamble all our life savings away at blackjack," she suggested whimsically.

"We could climb to the top of the Washington Monument," he quipped back.

"Ride a raft down the Potomac!"

"Stay up all night watching *Dragnet* reruns."

"Bake an eleven-layer cake."

"*Eat* an eleven-layer cake!"

They both laughed. Jonathan shook his head, dissatisfied. "I don't know. All those things sound like fun, but somehow they're not quite right for a first date. Know what I mean?"

"Yeah, I do." Lily felt warm all over even though the night breeze wafting in through the half-open windows of the truck was cool. Their first date did have to be something special. She knew Jonathan's expectations were as high as her own.

Jonathan had been frowning thoughtfully. Then suddenly his expression cleared. He turned to Lily with an eager but somewhat sheepish smile. "To heck with it," he declared, resting his left arm across the back of the seat behind Lily's head. "Maybe it's kind of heavy for a first date, but why don't we just go to the prom?"

Lily clapped her hands together, delighted. "The prom!" It was the last thing she'd expected to hear. And Jonathan was right, it *was* sort of heavy, but it was also sort of perfect.

"Will you go?" Jonathan waited for her answer.

"Go? I'd love to!" Lily leaned forward and gave Jonathan an impulsive hug. When she pulled back, she saw she'd left a smudge of white greasepaint on the shoulder of his orange T-shirt. "Oh, no!" she exlaimed, dismayed. She put a hand to her face. "I forgot I still had this stuff on! I don't know how you could take me seriously. How could you ask a girl whose face is painted like a clown to the prom?"

"Because I think she's beautiful," Jonathan said simply. "Because I've never liked a girl this way before."

Lily stared at him, her eyes wide. "Really?"

"Really." Jonathan slid over a little more from his side of the seat. Lily slid over a little from her direction. Now they were sitting very close to one another. Jonathan took off his fedora and deposited it on the dashboard. He leaned toward Lily, bumping his hand accidentally on the horn. Lily didn't laugh; instead she raised her face to his. They were both holding their breath. The instant their lips touched, Lily remembered her makeup. She pulled back reluctantly.

"Just a sec," she whispered, reaching into one of the grocery bags. She pulled out a paper napkin and used it to wipe at least some of the scarlet lipstick off her mouth. Then she smiled. Jonathan smiled back. "Now I'm ready," she said softly.

Jonathan lowered his arm from the back of the seat and curved it firmly around Lily's shoulders. He touched the tip of his nose to hers and then kissed her. This time Lily didn't move away. She wrapped her arms around Jonathan's neck and pulled him even closer.

The kiss was deep and warm. There were no fireworks, but somehow it felt even better to Lily that way. Everything about this moment felt so right. Jonathan's arms around her, his hand on her back, his mouth on hers, his hair thick and soft between her fingers, the way he smelled. Even the song on the radio, Van Morrison's "Crazy Love," was just right for the moment.

When they separated it was only because they wanted to gaze at each other for a while. Lily smiled when she saw what her kiss had done to Jonathan.

"Your face is *covered* with white greasepaint," she apologized.

"That's okay." He bent over and kissed her ear. "Your subs are getting soggy."

"That's okay."

They snuggled deeper in the seat. Lily knew she should get going to the cast party — everybody was going to wonder what happened to her. But as she and Jonathan kissed again, she decided she wanted to stay where she was, in his arms, for a whole lot longer.

Molly suddenly sat up straight. Her attention

was drawn to the sub shop entrance and a group of guys that had just come in. "Whoa. Now who is *that*?" she asked Frankie, who had returned from getting an order of fries.

Frankie grinned. "Oh, that's Zachary McGraw."

Josh, listening in on the conversation, did not smile. His eyes had clouded over and they only grew darker when Zachary, who was heading toward the counter with his friends from the track team to put in his order, spied Frankie. He made a beeline for the crowd's table.

Frankie greeted Zack with a friendly smile. At the same time, Molly sat up and tossed back her hair, clearly hoping Frankie would introduce her to this cute new hunk. Josh just glared at the other boy through his glasses. Zachary, however, only had eyes for Frankie. He was staring at her as if he'd never seen her before. "Hi, Franko, how's it going?"

"Hi, Zack." Frankie had to turn her back on Josh in order to face Zachary, who'd squatted down behind her, his incredibly blue eyes on a level with her own.

"It's nice bumping into you. I kind of miss you now that my tutoring is finished," he told her in a low voice.

"I . . . I miss you, too," she said, not quite sure how to respond to him. He wasn't speaking in the tone he usually used with her, the one-of-the-guys sort of approach. There was a new note in his voice that matched the new look in his eyes.

And he wasn't saying the sort of thing he used to say, either. "Did you change your hair or something?" he asked now. "I mean, it really looks good."

Frankie put a hand to the flowered challis scarf she'd knotted around her hair. "Yeah . . . kind of," she stuttered.

Zack was shaking his head, puzzled. "Nope, it's not just the hair. Something about you looks different. I don't know what it is." He smiled approvingly.

Frankie blushed. She did look different; she recognized it herself when she looked in the mirror. She knew a lot of it had to do with the way she'd felt about herself since she fell in love with Josh. As her mom said, being in love gave you the kind of glow you couldn't get from make-up. Zack wasn't the first person to comment on it, but he was the last person she'd expected to notice. It hadn't been very long ago that Zack had been so infatuated with Holly Daniels that he wouldn't have noticed Frankie if she dyed her hair green.

Zack didn't seem to observe Frankie's surprise and confusion. Neither of them saw Molly's raised eyebrows or Josh's grim frown. "Well, I should probably get back to my buddies," he said, sounding as if he'd really rather stay and talk with Frankie. "If I leave them alone with that food for too long there won't be anything left for me!"

Frankie smiled, hiding her relief. "I'll see you around."

Zack smiled back, a sweet, serious expression in his eyes. "I really hope so," he said earnestly. "So long."

" 'Bye."

Zachary got to his feet and headed for the booth

his friends had piled into. Before anyone, even a visibly peeved Josh, could comment on Zachary's visit, Jonathan rejoined them. His eyes were dreamy and unfocused; he was clearly floating somewhere up around Cloud Nine.

Matt rubbed his chin, his mouth twisting in a half-smile. "Got a little white makeup on your face there, Preston," he teased.

"And is that lipstick I see?" Greg pointed a plastic straw at the red smudges on Jonathan's cheeks and chin. Jonathan merely grinned.

"Yeah. Is she the reason we've hardly seen you lately?" Molly leaned her elbows on the table and rested her chin in her hands. Her eyes sparkled with curiosity. "And who *is* she, anyway?"

Jonathan's forehead wrinkled. "Didn't I tell you?"

"No!" the crowd yelled in unison.

"She's new, from Stevenson," he explained proudly. "Her name's Lily Rorshack. She was in *The Fantasticks.*"

Jonathan wasn't sure how he'd expected his friends to react. Maybe not stand on their heads and burst into song — after all, he assumed they knew as little about Lily as he had when he met her. Whatever he'd expected, however, he wasn't prepared for the heavy, stunned silence.

"*Lily Rorshack*?" Brian repeated, an undercurrent of something like anger coloring his voice. Molly and Frankie exchanged a nervous glance. Eric's mouth had dropped open in astonishment, and Greg dropped his straw.

"Yes, Lily Rorshack," Jonathan affirmed, slightly confused.

"Lily *Rorshack*?" Now it was Karen who expressed her utter disbelief.

"That's what I said!" Jonathan exclaimed, irritated. "What's everybody's problem? You'd think I just confessed that I was hanging around with the Bride of Frankenstein! What's so horrible about Lily Rorshack?"

Elise looked at Karen and Brian. "Don't you know about what Lily did?" she asked Jonathan.

Jonathan got a sick, mad feeling in his stomach. "Apparently not," he snapped.

"Come on, where've you been?" Greg challenged him. "It was practically all anybody talked about for days . . . weeks! I can't believe she was here. And we didn't even realize it was her!"

"Look, I don't know what you're talking about," Jonathan protested. "If you think Lily has something to do with this ridiculous feud — "

"Something to *do* with it?" Brian laughed harshly. "Man, she practically started it!"

Jonathan went pale. "Exactly what do you mean by that?"

Brian related the story about how Karen had interviewed Lily and then printed the interview in *The Red and the Gold*. And after that, Lily even repeated her story on *WKND*.

"Wait a minute, I think I remember that much," Jonathan interrupted.

"Yeah, well, it's what happened next that may interest you now," Brian assured him. "It was after Karen went ahead and entered her article about Lily in that journalism contest that we found out, thanks to Frankie, that Lily was lying through the whole interview. She'd never been a runaway *or* a street kid. She never reformed from anything! She and Daniel Tackett just put together that interview as a practical joke on Karen and Elise and everybody on the paper. Everybody at Kennedy! Very funny, huh? It almost ruined Karen's college journalism career."

Jonathan was speechless. He knew from Brian's impassioned tone that he was telling the truth. The expressions on his other friends' faces — all a combination of dismay and compassion — only served to confirm it.

"I can't believe you didn't know," Molly said, trying not to look him straight in the eyes.

"I . . . I've been busy," Jonathan mumbled, his voice cracking.

"Too busy to know that those Stevenson kids are creeps?" Everyone turned in surprise. Ordinarily mild-mannered Josh was red with indignation. "They're creeps," he repeated, blustering. He glanced aggressively in the direction of Zachary's table, his hand pounding the table. "We shouldn't have anything to do with them."

Frankie looked at Josh in complete surprise. Josh avoided her eyes.

The atmosphere at the table had been tense, and now it was downright uncomfortable. The entire group had gone silent, and everyone was staring at their unfinished milk shakes and subs. Jonathan sank down on the bench, wishing he could sink down into the floor. So that's what the feud had been all about, he thought dully. Lily was part of it; Lily was right smack in the middle of it. He pictured Lily's face — sweet, playful, innocent. It didn't seem to fit. But then, she was an actress. She could probably be anything she wanted if it suited her, if it worked in with her hurtful jokes and schemes.

Suddenly Jonathan couldn't sit still amid the strained silence any longer. He untangled his legs from the bench and left without meeting anyone's eyes. No one followed him as he rushed out to the back parking lot to where his '57 Chevy convertible was parked. He climbed in and just sat there for a few long minutes, resting his head on his arms on top of the steering wheel. His mind was racing with conflicting and confusing thoughts and emotions. Lily Rorshack was a liar, a con artist. She might also be pretty and appealing and magical, but those qualities couldn't rescue her from Brian's accusations. The evidence all pointed in one direction: Lily hated Kennedy High School and everyone associated with it. And just a few minutes before, Jonathan had let her fool him into thinking she really cared for him! Lily was probably out to use him — to lead him on, only for Jonathan to find out that all her words were lies. He beat the palm of his hand against the steering wheel, hurt and frustrated. What a mistake it had been to let his defenses down. He should have learned after Fiona, and Roxanne. Especially Roxanne!

Jonathan started Big Pink's engine and pulled out of the parking lot a little too fast. He narrowed his eyes against the cool night wind, and against the realization that no matter how painful it would be, he had to break things off with Lily. It was over with her, before it had even really begun.

Chapter 8

Molly flopped down on the exercise mat. She tucked her right leg, bent at the knee, behind her while extending her left out in front. "It was absolutely horrible," she assured Katie, twisting a few times at the waist before stretching forward to grip the toes of her left foot with both hands. "You should have seen Jonathan's face. I thought he was going to cry or hit somebody or something."

Molly had joined Katie before her next gymnastics meet in a pre-warm-up warm-up. In ten minutes Katie, as captain, would be leading her teammates in a team warm-up in Kennedy's main gym, but for now the two girls had the smaller exercise room all to themselves. Katie paused in her own stretching as Molly finished telling her about the scene at the sub shop on Saturday night. "Poor Jonathan," Katie said finally. She swung her legs out in a Chinese split and then bent forward at the waist, her chest touching the mat. "I mean, I don't trust some of the Stevenson kids any more than the rest of you do, but I still feel badly for him. I can't believe he didn't know the story about the interview! And I thought *I* was out of touch."

"I guess Jonathan's been so preoccupied with organizing stuff lately — that May Day thing, Greg's campaign, the prom — you know, getting the big picture, that he hasn't been able to see a lot of what's going on right under his nose," Molly suggested.

"What do you think he'll do?" Katie wondered.

"I don't know. He hasn't known her long enough to feel really strongly about her, has he? And considering what he knows about her now, I can't imagine he could like her the way he did before."

Katie straightened up with a sigh. It was depressing to hear about someone else's romantic problems — it reminded her of her own stonewalled relationship. Not that she really needed reminding. Katie thought about Greg and about everything that had gone wrong between them as much, if not more, than she used to think about him when they were together and going strong. Doesn't love work out for anybody? she thought sadly. Out loud to Molly she said, "So other than *that* how was your Saturday night?"

Molly laughed wryly, abandoning her workout to sit with her knees tucked up under her, watching Katie. "Other than that I guess it was okay. A bunch of us had been planning to head over to Rockers to hear a band that Brian said was good. But somehow after the Lily thing, no one really felt like staying out late so we canned it." She bent over to retie the laces on one of her sneakers, her dark hair falling over her face.

When she looked up again her expression had become a little bit wistful. "We — uh — you know we miss you hanging around us," she said, even though she knew she was entering awkward and sensitive territory.

"I miss you guys, too." Katie did her best to sound upbeat, hiding her feelings by turning away from Molly to lie on her side for leg lifts. She missed being a part of things even more than Molly, the most supportive of friends, could know.

"It's not as much fun without you," Molly continued. She saw Katie's back stiffen and added contritely, "Sorry, K.C. I didn't say that to make you feel guilty. I understand . . . we all understand. We want you to get back into the swing of things."

"Thanks, Moll," Katie said in a small voice.

Molly was fiddling with the lace on her other sneaker now. "Yeah, well, I hope you do . . . before we graduate, 'cause then we'll just have this summer to hang out. Wow! College."

Katie sighed. "No kidding!"

Molly suddenly remembered something that she thought might cheer Katie up. "I almost forgot! Greg asked about you at the sub shop."

Katie sat up and faced Molly, her heart giving a hopeful leap in spite of everything. Molly knew Greg and Katie weren't speaking to one another and was constantly looking for ways to reconcile them. Katie was ordinarily wary of her friend's efforts, but she couldn't help being curious. "What'd he say?" she asked.

Molly frowned. "I'm not sure. Something like, 'How's Katie these days?' "

" 'How's Katie these days?' " Katie repeated, a wave of bitterness sweeping over her. "That's the kind of thing you ask about somebody you knew ages ago, someone you don't plan on seeing very often anymore."

Molly shook her head firmly. "That's not true, Katie," she argued. "You know it's not. He cares about you as much as he ever did. If you don't believe in anything else, you should believe that!"

"Don't you think I believe in anything?" Katie challenged. She had to bite her lips to keep the angry, forlorn tears from her eyes.

Molly softened. "I didn't mean it that way. I think you believe in a lot of things. You always did and you still do. Most of all, you've got to keep believing — "

"I know, I know." Katie cut her off as she jumped to her feet. "I've got to believe in myself."

"I wasn't trying to preach," Molly said, sounding hurt.

"I know you weren't." Katie retrieved her team warm-up jacket from where she'd draped it on a set of uneven bars, and then turned back to Molly. "I'm sorry I snapped at you," she apologized sincerely. "You're right, about believing in myself. It *is* the most important thing. And I'm trying, I really am. And you know" — she managed a genuinely optimistic smile — "I'm feeling better about myself all the time."

The two girls just looked at each other for a

long moment. Then, at the same time, they stepped forward to hug one another. Katie laughed. "What a couple of saps," she said, wiping a stray tear from her cheek.

"I know, it's really disgusting!" Molly faked a sniffle and then grinned.

Katie looked at her watch. "I've got to run," she said. "Are you going to stick around and watch the meet?"

Molly nodded, her dark curls bouncing. "Yep. I thought I'd run a few laps on the track outside first, though. But I'll see you later."

"Okay."

The two girls walked to the door of the exercise room together. As they parted to go their separate ways, Molly called back to Katie. "Break a leg!" Then she stopped and smacked her forehead.

Katie giggled. "Not the other one, too!"

Molly started laughing, too. "I *meant* 'go for it!' "

"Gotcha." Katie waved good-bye. As she trotted toward the gym for the team's warm-up, she thought her broken leg — her *healed* broken leg — felt stronger than it had before the last gymnastics meet. She had a feeling today's showing against Maryville was going to be an improvement over Carrolton. Things were looking up.

After her conversation with Molly, Katie felt strangely at ease. The fear and nervousness she'd experienced before the last meet, her first time back in competition, was gone. She'd faced the worst that day: The reality that she'd lost her old form and that it would be a long time and a lot of hard work before she got it back again. She'd faced this and accepted it. She didn't have a choice. And she decided she might as well accept it graciously. Besides, there was something else she could do well, a way she could still contribute something to the team.

Katie and Stacy had been working together regularly since their first "coaching" session after the last meet, which made Katie feel good, since for so many months she had been completely aggravated by the giddy, unserious sophomore. After the team's daily workout, with the enthusiastic approval of Ms. Muldoon, the two stayed on in the gym for an extra hour of private practice. Sometimes they spent most of the hour gabbing, but even that helped a little, Katie thought. Stacy might never feel the dedication to gymnastics that Katie herself had possessed for years, but the bubbly sophomore was definitely developing a new, more mature perspective. All in all, Katie thought she saw an improvement in Stacy's performance every day. The meet today would tell for certain, though.

When it was time for Katie to do her floor exercise, she approached the mats calmly. The excitement was there — competing was what she loved best — but she'd taken the pressure off herself. She wasn't out there to win, which had always been her primary motivation. Now she just wanted to do better than her last time out. Right as she was about to start her routine she saw Greg slide over next to Molly in the bleachers, and she felt a few butterflies start up in her stomach. Stop right there! she commanded silently, willing the butterflies to be still. Take Greg's support for what it is — just support. For old time's sake.

The routine went smoothly. While she was conscious that she was still favoring her weak leg, Katie was physically looser and more confident than she'd been at any time since the ski accident. When she finished she knew that she'd improved a little, even though her performance had still been just fair. Just fair by her standards, but good enough to be the sixth best score so far.

Katie didn't dwell on her showing. Instead, she focused all her mental energy on some last-minute coaching with Stacy. The two girls huddled together behind the Kennedy team's pile of towels and warm-up suits. "You looked good," Stacy told Katie, mumbling through the bobby pins she gripped in her teeth.

"Thanks. I felt a lot more relaxed today." Katie bent over to massage her right calf muscle. "How about you? Are you psyched? You're up next!"

Stacy placed the last bobby pin in her hair and then pretended to nibble her nails nervously. "Gee, Coach, I just don't know if I can handle all the heat! Is it too late to try out for the Trivial Pursuit team instead?"

Katie giggled. "Aren't you ever going to be serious?"

"Probably not!" Stacy said brightly. "*More* serious, maybe. Even *relatively* serious. But never just plain *serious*."

Katie shook her head in mock dismay. " 'And she shows so much promise,' " she intoned in the deepest voice she could muster. "Anyway, Stacy, remember what I told you about not untucking too soon during your flip? And hold those landings just a fraction of a second longer so they're crisper."

Stacy nodded. "And point my toes more."

"Keep your chin up when you're running."

"And my shoulders back."

Katie caught Stacy's gaze straying to the bleachers to search for her friends. "And most of all, *concentrate*!" she added firmly.

Stacy turned back to her with a laugh. "Right."

"Have fun!"

Katie held her breath as Stacy, again the last gymnast to perform on the floor, began her exercise. When it really got down to it, there was only so much her coaching could do. Most of what it would take to be a winner had to come from inside Stacy herself.

Amazingly, Stacy was showing that she did have what it took. There were still a lot of rough edges in her routine, but the overall effect had improved incredibly.

After her final landing, Stacy sprinted over to Katie and started bouncing up and down like a pogo stick. Even before her score of 8.75 was announced, she knew, and so did Katie, that she'd done well. "I did it! I did it!" she exclaimed with a joyous toss of her ponytail.

Katie beamed. "You placed third, Stacy! All right!"

Stacy collapsed in a laughing heap on one of the folding chairs. "I can't believe it," she said breathlessly. "I never thought I'd actually earn a point for the team."

"Well, you did. And I'll bet it's the first of many." Katie was a little surprised at herself. Stacy was just on the brink of what could be a stellar career with the Kennedy gymnastics team, while Katie's own best days were behind her. She should be envious, but she wasn't in the least. She didn't resent Stacy's success; she felt a part of it. "You were great," she told the other girl sincerely.

"Thanks." Stacy pulled the elastic from her hair and shook her head. Then she squinted at Katie. "I mean it, really. Thank you. I couldn't have done it without you."

Katie shrugged, but she was pleased. "I'm just glad I could help."

"You did — a lot. And, K.C. . . ." Stacy hesitated. "Do you think maybe we could keep on working together? I mean, maybe not every day, but now and then? I feel like I still have a whole lot to learn."

Katie eyed her skeptically. "You're serious? You really want to?"

Stacy grinned. "Well, I'm *relatively* serious."

Katie laughed. "Okay, you're on!"

A few minutes later Katie chalked up her hands for the uneven bars, her heart light. It made her feel good to know Stacy appreciated her assistance. No, not good, terrific. She'd enjoyed Stacy's third-place triumph almost as much as if it were her own. And in a way it was.

Katie felt a lot of the old charge as she swung into her routine on the bars. Whether she won or lost, she was back where she should be. Whether she won or lost, she was still a success.

Mr. Barclay tugged on his droopy, sand-colored mustache and cleared his throat loudly. "Ahem. Ms. Rorshack, I am aware that you were a participant in the school musical, but I wish to remind you that we are discussing *King Lear* which, to my knowledge, has not yet been set to music."

Lily snapped out of her daydream, realizing with a start that she had been whistling a tuneless rendition of "Crazy Love." The entire class was grinning. She shifted her focus from the waving branches of the elm tree outside the classroom window to her teacher's long face. "Sorry, Mr. Barclay," she apologized with what she hoped was an appropriately penitent expression. "I guess I have spring fever."

He frowned. "Well, try to catch a little Shakespeare fever, will you?"

Lily nodded, but as soon as Mr. Barclay resumed his discussion of Act II, scene iii, she turned her eyes back to the open window. It was a fresh, clear day, the kind of weather you wished would last forever. Of course, it never did. The Kennedy High grounds crew had just mowed the lawn and the sweet scent of cut grass was almost more than Lily could bear. She wanted to kick off her sandals and run outside in bare feet. She definitely had spring fever, but she knew her happily dazed state was the result of something more than just the season. I'm in love, she thought, enjoying the way the word echoed around inside her head. She would have liked to say it out loud, but then Mr. Barclay would really think she was bonkers. I'm in love! Well, not *really*, she admitted silently. Falling in love took more than one kiss. But one kiss could sort of get it started. That's what she was experiencing, she decided, love starting. Starting out small maybe, but *starting*.

She looked down at her open spiral notebook. The page was blank except for the heading "*King Lear*, Act II." Lily hadn't taken a single note yesterday or today. She would be in serious trouble when it came time for Friday's weekly quiz. Oh, well, she thought, touching her pen to the paper. It's too late to start paying attention to old Lear now. She drew a big heart right in the center of the page, decorated it with scalloped edging, and then wrote "L.R. + J.P." in the middle. Then she crossed it out thoroughly in case anyone was reading over her shoulder. Which she decided was unlikely since she was sitting in the back row. So she drew another heart. She was beginning to wonder if last period English would ever end, when the bell rang. Twenty-two students catapulted out of their chairs and toward the door with Lily in their midst.

Once she was in the hall, Lily strolled at a leisurely pace to her locker, then took her time getting her books together. She pulled her oversized jacket on slowly. Moving at such a snail's pace was a real effort; she would have preferred to run. But she figured it would be a good idea to give Greg's friends — and she supposed Greg himself — time to get to his headquarters before she arrived to offer to join the campaign.

Lily hadn't seen or spoken to Jonathan in three days, not since they said good-night on Saturday, embracing in the cab of her truck. But she hadn't stopped thinking about him for a second. His kisses and his words — everything about him — had made a deep impression on her. She was more excited than she would have thought possible at the prospect of spending time with him again and getting to know him better. There was the prom to look forward to, too. She wouldn't have thought she'd ever get so excited about something so . . . *high schoolish.* But she was. She even couldn't wait to buy a dress. What style, though? she wondered. Should she go funky or Victorian; sophisticated or simple? Well whatever she decided on, it would definitely make a statement.

Lily was also getting psyched to see Jonathan's friends again. They seemed so easygoing. The next time she saw them, she'd really make an effort to make them her friends, too. It just went to show, not that Lily really needed the proof, how wrong Roxanne Easton could be.

In fact, the more Lily compared Jonathan and his crowd to Roxanne and her own loosely knit Stevenson group, the more she felt that Roxanne's and Daniel's criticisms of the Kennedy leaders were unjustified. If anything, it was Rox and Daniel who were sour and uncompromising. Lily hadn't been thrilled when Daniel had been pushed forward as the presidential candidate who would represent the interests of the Stevenson kids. She'd almost rather Rox herself ran! It didn't take much to see that whatever crowd he belonged to, Greg Montgomery was far and away the best candidate. And if he just so happened to be one of Jonathan's best friends, so much the better! All the more reason, Lily had decided, to support him.

Entering the stairwell on her way to Room 205, she smiled as she pictured the look on Roxanne's face when she found out Lily had defected to the enemy camp. She wasn't defying her Stevenson friends just to spite Rox, but she had to admit that was one more incentive. Lily started climbing the stairs one at a time, but by the time she was halfway up she couldn't restrain herself any longer. She knew Jonathan, as Greg's campaign manager, was sure to be at headquarters and she simply couldn't wait to see him.

She took the last four steps in two jumps, and flew through the door into the upper hall as if she'd been shot through a cannon. She skidded around a corner and to a stop in front of Room 205, panting slightly. The door was closed — good! As an actress, Lily knew how important it was to make an entrance. She took a few seconds to comb her fingers through her hair, fluffing it up, and to adjust the wide leather belt that cinched the soft denim jumpsuit at her hips. Then she knocked eagerly on the door.

"Hey!" "Come in!" "Yo!" an assortment of voices called out.

Lily swung the door open and breezed through, an animated smile lighting up her face. There were about a dozen people in the room, and she didn't see Jonathan right away. The first people to acknowledge Lily's cheerful "Hi, everybody!" were Karen and Brian, who were standing just inside the door. They were busy rolling up a huge red-and-gold felt GREG MONTGOMERY FOR PRESIDENT banner, and to say they didn't exactly greet her with open arms would be the understatement of the year. They had been laughing together, but when they saw Lily, the smiles disappeared from their faces. Karen didn't even say hello. Instead, she turned her back and resumed her work on the banner. Brian merely grunted, then did the same.

Lily stood rooted to the spot, completely taken aback. Weren't these the same people she'd seen a few nights ago? It made a little sense that Karen and Brian might be a little less than warm, but what about the others? She was here to help. Then it struck her. Knowing she was part of the *Stevenson* crowd, they probably thought she was spying on them for Daniel. All she had to do was tell them she was on their side and everything would be fine.

Instantly relieved, she approached the next person she saw. It was Elise, and just beyond her were Adam and Molly. "Hi," she tried again, addressing all three. "I just stopped by to see if I could . . . I'd really like to help with Greg's campaign. Do you guys have any work I could do?"

Once again Lily was met with an icy, inexplicable silence. Elise only looked up from the poster she was designing to give Lily a steely glare. Adam, clearly uncomfortable, pretended to study Elise's poster. Molly was left holding the ball. "Um . . . uh, I don't know," she mumbled, darting an uncertain glance toward the rear of the room.

Lily followed the direction of Molly's eyes. In a small alcove in a back corner was a desk, and at the desk Jonathan and Greg were sitting side by side. The panicky feeling that had stolen into Lily's stomach and heart melted at the sight of Jonathan's familiar face. She hurried over to him, eager to escape the strangely tense atmosphere of the rest of the room.

The two boys were flipping through some computer printouts together. Greg looked up with a guarded expression on his face when Lily stopped in front of the desk, but Jonathan kept his head bent.

"Sorry to interrupt," she began hopefully. "I just wanted — "

Greg interrupted her. "Jonathan is my campaign manager. If you have anything to discuss, you may speak with him. Thanks for stopping by." Then he got quickly to his feet, looking almost embarrassed, and headed for the front of the room. With Greg gone, Jonathan had to look up, but even so he managed to avoid meeting Lily's eyes.

"Hey, Jonathan," Lily said softly. "I'm glad I found you! What are you working on?"

"A draft of Greg's convention speech," he answered, his voice flat.

Lily gulped. She tried to joke, even though she was no longer in a very playful mood. " 'When in the course of human events' . . . something like that?"

"Yeah, something like that." Jonathan had resumed his perusal of the speech. Lily stared at the top of his head. Did she have to spell out the reason for her presence to Jonathan, too?

"I . . . I'm here because I wondered. . . ." Lily faltered. "I was hoping I could get involved in Greg's campaign."

Jonathan clenched his teeth, his jawline hardening. "We don't need any more volunteers," he informed her bluntly.

Lily's jaw dropped. After her strange reception from the other kids in the room she was ready for almost anything. But not this. She stared at Jonathan, who faced her again, although he seemed to be focusing on her left ear rather than her eyes. She would never have expected rudeness and utterly impersonal behavior from the boy she had shared such a special moment with the other night. "Is it . . . is it because I'm friends with Daniel Tackett?" she stuttered, clutching at straws in an attempt to understand why Jonathan was acting this way.

He acted as if he hadn't heard her question, and maybe he hadn't. His mind had obviously moved to another subject. When he spoke again, it was to drop an even bigger bombshell on an already demoralized Lily. "And by the way," he phrased it as an afterthought, "something's come up. I have to cancel for the prom. Sorry."

Lily's arms went limp at her sides. She was too stunned to notice that Jonthan's hands shook as he shuffled the pages of Greg's speech into a neat stack. His words, his tone, his manner, all had left her mute and paralyzed. Lily felt as if this were some terrible nightmare — a play where she'd forgotten all her lines, or maybe never even learned them to begin with.

Jonathan was breathing hard, in an effort it seemed to keep from saying any more. Lily suddenly came to life. Without a word, she spun on the heels of her flat brown boots and ran. She couldn't see the expressions on the faces of his friends as she passed them, but she was glad. She was sure they were gloating at having chased the Stevenson girl away.

Once she was safely out of Room 205, Lily still didn't stop running. She didn't stop until she reached the stairwell at the end of the hall. Inside, she sat down on the cold concrete top step, her legs trembling too much to carry her farther. As the tears started down her cheeks, she buried her face in her arms, a desperate sob catching at her throat.

She didn't understand what had just happened. Why would Jonathan want to hurt her? What had she done wrong? She'd gone to Stevenson, that was what was wrong. Was it because of the mock interview she'd done with Karen and Brian? Her "street persona" act?

And Jonathan had asked her to the prom!

A cold, bitter taste stole into Lily's aching throat. It must all have been a mean joke. Jonathan probably never meant to take her to the prom in the first place. He and all his friends probably got a good chuckle out of her naivete. Lily, the class cut-up, only now it was their turn to laugh. A new flood of tears streamed down her face. It looked like Roxanne had been right about "the crowd" all along.

Chapter 10

After school the day before the mock convention, the whole crowd crammed into Greg's campaign headquarters. There they put together last-minute publicity items to distribute in the halls and in the field house, where the convention woud take place. Holly, Diana, and Jeremy struggled with the hand-operated button-making machine, while Elise, assisted by a rainbow of wide markers, wrote VOTE FOR GREG MONTGOMERY on sheets of poster board. Adam and Matt then stapled them to wooden "T's" to make signs. Meanwhile, Karen and Jonathan brainstormed slogans, hoping to come up with something catchy for Greg's supporters to chant. Molly, Eric, and Frankie had been collaborating on text for a one-page handout. Now Frankie, who was seated at the computer they'd borrowed from the student government room, printed out the draft. Eric retrieved it from the printer and handed it to Molly, who handed it back to him. So he handed it to Frankie, who scanned it rapidly.

"Well, *I* think it's okay," she said. "All Greg's points are pretty clear." She held it out at arm's length and studied it, her head tipped thoughtfully to one side. "Although I still think it could be shorter, punchier."

"Maybe we need another opinion," Eric suggested, tapping out a drum beat on top of the computer monitor.

"Three wasn't enough?" Molly joked.

"I know." Frankie folded the sheet and jumped to her feet. "I'll run over to WKND and see what Josh has to say. He hasn't been staring at it for an hour like we have — maybe he'll have some ideas."

On her way to the radio station, Frankie realized it had been a while since she'd visited Josh there. With things gearing up for the convention, she'd been spending a lot of her free time at Greg's headquarters instead. It was fun working on the campaign, but she would be sort of glad when it was over — as long as Greg won, that is. Then it would be election day, and that night, the prom! There'd be a lot to celebrate, and she and Josh could do it together.

Frankie was smiling in anticipation as she pushed open the door marked WKND. There was nobody in the outer office, but she could see Brian in the record closet. She crossed the room and peeked in at him. "What're you doing?" she asked, looking over his shoulder at the list he was scribbling on his clipboard.

Brian wiped his forehead with the back of one hand and raised his eyebrows. "Record inventory," he explained. "Fun, fun, fun!"

Frankie looked around the cramped closet as if she expected to see Josh materialize from between two album covers. "Where's Josh? Shouldn't he be helping you?"

Brian sat back on his heels, running a hand over his short dark hair. "I'm not sure where he is, but I think I can guess." He looked at the floor, then back up at her. "Frankie, have you noticed that Josh has been acting sort of . . . strange lately?"

Frankie sat down on a stack of albums, pulling her pink knit dress down over her knees. "How do you mean?" she asked, puzzled.

"Well, this whole body-building kick." Brian resumed his inventory.

Frankie raised her pale eyebrows. "A body-building kick?" she repeated. Body building and Josh were such a weird combination that she couldn't help laughing out loud.

"Yeah, it's really bizarre. I mean, Jane Fonda never took exercise this seriously! For the last week or so, every free minute he's been sneaking off to the gym or the track. A couple of times he's pumped iron so hard he could barely move to push the buttons in the booth the next day!"

"I had no idea!" Frankie frowned. "That really doesn't sound like Josh."

Brian shook his head. "You're telling me. But I bet if you go out to the football field right now, you'll find him running laps like a marine corps recruit."

She was already on her way to the door. "I'll do that," she said, waving good-bye over her shoulder. "See you later, Brian!"

Frankie was completely mystified. Maybe she *had* noticed that Josh hadn't been quite himself lately. He'd been a little cranky, even terse on a few occasions, but she'd assumed he was just feeling a little pressured by his extracurricular activities and the thought of final exams coming up soon. This new obsession with exercise, though, was really odd, the last sort of obsession she would have imagined Josh developing. But what was oddest was that he hadn't said a word about it. It just wasn't like him to keep something like that from her.

Frankie exited from the south wing of the school, coming out at the edge of the spring-green lawn bordering the football field and stands. She walked gingerly, the heels of her new pink pumps sinking into the grass with every step. As she approached it, she could see the cinder track was bustling with activity. The track team was in the midst of its workout and there were a few dozen runners dashing about, not to mention the clutter of hurdles, starting blocks, and field event equipment. Frankie squinted against the hazy afternoon sun, brushing back a strand of hair the breeze had blown across her face. She didn't see Josh anywhere, but then it occurred to her that she probably wouldn't recognize him anyway. She'd never seen Josh in anything but his regular clothes. She peered at the runners, looking for someone in faded cords, funky hightops, and horn-rimmed glasses.

Just then the wind snatched the draft for Greg's flyer out of Frankie's hand. It sailed twenty-five yards or so and came to rest against a thick high jump mat, which had been set up on the grass behind a small equipment storage shed. Frankie ran after the paper, curling her toes so she wouldn't lose her shoes. She bent over to retrieve it, and when she stood up, nearly bumped into a boy who'd come up behind her.

She was expecting Josh but it was Zachary. She let out a startled gasp and stepped backward, nearly collapsing on the mat. Zachary put out a firm hand on her arm to steady her. "Sorry, there! Didn't mean to scare you."

"That's okay," Frankie assured him. She'd recovered her balance, but she noticed that Zack didn't let go of her arm. Not only that, he was looking at her in the same funny way he'd looked at her at the sub shop. The look that would make her think, if she didn't know better, that he was attracted to her.

What he said next astonished her even more than the expression in his eyes or the pressure of his fingers on her skin. "I was working out," he began, nodding at a row of hurdles set up along the section of the track that wasn't blocked from their view by the shed, "and I saw you. I came right over." He smiled warmly at Frankie and she smiled hesitantly back. Zack was silent for a moment, as if he were considering how to phrase what he was going to say next, and then he blurted, "I'm glad you came out here. I've been looking for you, too. I wanted to tell you . . . I finally realized how you feel about me and I feel the same way about you."

Zachary blushed and Frankie went pale. She opened her mouth to protest, but he plunged back into his speech before she had a chance to. "I know we've been friends for a long time. We've gone through a lot together, haven't we, Franko? Transferring to Kennedy and all — "

"Zack, I — "

"I'm not sure why it took me so long to notice you. I mean, not so much to notice you but to . . . you know, *notice* you." He grinned shyly. Frankie just stared at him, her eyes as wide as saucers. Zack couldn't have taken her more by surprise if he'd told her he was shaving off all his hair and joining a monastery.

Frankie shook her head, trying to gather her wits back together. She would have simply chickened out and run away, but Zack had her unintentionally but thoroughly cornered against the high jump mat. She knew she had to say something to set him straight, and fast. "But I thought you liked Holly. And I like — "

"I'm over Holly," Zachary insisted, his eyes earnest. "I'm way over her. You're the one I think about now, all the time. About how nice you've always been to me, the tutoring, all the times I needed someone to talk to. . . . You're wonderful, Franko. I'm wild about you!"

Frankie was stunned. She couldn't have run away now even if Zachary had stepped aside and cleared her a path. Her legs were paralyzed, and she felt like her heart had stopped beating. No boy had ever talked to her, gushed over her, quite like this — not even Josh. It was flattering and overwhelming. And it also felt wrong. Frankie knew she shouldn't have let Zack say these things to her when she had a boyfriend and wasn't free to respond to him the way he'd like her to. But he'd said them and now she struggled to find the words to answer him. Her brain whirled. She had to tell him that she was involved with someone else, that whatever she'd felt for him once had gone. If his feelings had changed, well, so had hers — only in the opposite direction.

But even as Frankie thought all this, she was still as aware as ever, if in an altered, somehow distanced way, of how incredibly good-looking Zachary was. She'd fantasized so many times back in the days of her hopeless crush on him that he would stand in front of her like this and say these things to her. And then he'd take her into his strong arms and kiss her. . . .

Before Frankie had a chance to separate past fantasy from present reality, Zachary *had* taken her in his arms. He pulled her close, and although she kept her hand braced against his broad, hard chest, she didn't push him away. She could feel the heat of his skin through his damp T-shirt, and suddenly his nearness fascinated her, electrified her. When he bent his head to kiss her, she turned her lips automatically toward his. The moment was exactly the way Frankie had always imagined it would be. Zachary's arms were strong and his mouth was warm. But the most important element was missing. There was no spark of caring, at least on her side. Where once her heart might have thumped like crazy, now it was just beating normally.

Frankie suddenly went cold inside from her nose to her toes. She pulled back abruptly from Zack's embrace so she could look him right in the eyes. Frankie had to think clearly. She tested herself: What do I feel? The answer was *nothing*. All at once a wave of relief tinged with regret and guilt washed over her. Regret because she didn't want to hurt Zachary's feelings, but it looked like she was going to have to. Relief because as she stared at Zachary's gorgeous face she was more sure than ever that Josh was the boy, the only boy, for her. Guilt because if Josh knew she'd kissed another guy, even by accident —

Just then Frankie heard someone gasp behind her. It can't be, she thought as she whirled around, shaking Zachary's hands from where they still gripped her shoulders. But it was. It was Josh, his dark hair soaked with sweat from running laps and his eyes so full of pain that it hurt Frankie just to look at them. Her mouth went dry, and she had to lick her lips before she could speak. "Josh, I — I mean, we — "

"Can explain?" he filled in for her, his voice hoarse. "I'll bet you can, but don't bother! I don't need to hear it — I can see it. You really wanted to go out with this jock all along, didn't you? I was okay until someone better came along." Frankie took a step toward him, but he waved her back with an angry gesture. "Look, you've got what you want, let's just leave it at that!

Forget the prom . . . forget everything!" Josh's voice cracked as if he were choking on the bitter words. "I hope you two are *very happy* together!"

After this parting shot, Josh stormed away, disappearing around the corner of the shed. Frankie could tell he was walking extra straight and tall, in an attempt to disguise the fact that he was very near tears. She herself now sank in a heap on the high jump mat, tears flowing freely.

When Josh first started his tirade, Zachary had drawn a complete blank on him. He wasn't sure he'd ever seen the other guy before, associated with Frankie or otherwise. By the time Josh finished, however, he would have to be a fool not to realize there was some sort of serious relationship between the two of them.

Now he knelt on the mat next to the distraught Frankie. "Franko . . . hey, Franko, shh." He put an arm around her shoulders and gave her a squeeze, but Frankie kept on crying, her hands pressed to her face. Zack ran a hand over his own face, confused. "Franko, what just happened? Who was that guy? What'd I do?"

Through her sniffles, Frankie managed to explain to him that Josh was — or at least had been — her boyfriend. Hearing this, Zack slapped his palm against his forehead, his confused expression giving way to one of self-disgust. "I did it again!" he moaned. "Just like I did with Holly. When I fell for her, I didn't know she was seeing anybody. Thanks to my stupidity, her and what's-his-name practically broke up. I can't believe I did it again." He bent over Frankie, awkwardly trying to wipe her tear-streaked cheeks with the bandanna he'd pulled from the back pocket of his shorts. "I'm so sorry, Franko. I never meant to make trouble for you. Please stop crying."

Frankie shook her head. "No." She made a noise that was half-hiccup, half-sob. "I can't." She really didn't think she could.

"Aw, geez." Zachary's eyebrows wrinkled in distress. "Franko, what can I do to make up for getting you into this dumb mess? I know, the prom. Will you go with me? I was going to ask you anyway . . . before . . . when — "

Frankie shook her head. "That's okay," she said. She took a deep, shaky breath, trying to control the tears that were still welling slowly in her eyes. She might as well stop crying, now that she thought about it. Crying wouldn't change anything. Crying couldn't erase the last ten minutes. "It's okay," she assured Zachary again, even though it wasn't. She wiped her eyes with his bandanna and then handed it back to him. "Thanks for asking but . . . I don't think I want to go to the prom anymore."

She had been studying her short, neat fingernails. Now she looked at Zachary, and the caring and concern in his eyes made her own eyes watery again. No, she didn't want to go to the prom with Zack. If she couldn't go with Josh she didn't want to go with anyone. And it looked like she wasn't going to the prom, or anywhere, with Josh, ever again.

Chapter 11

Wednesday was a half day at Kennedy so that the mock convention could get started right after lunch. Lily dove from the cafeteria into the flood of students pouring through the hallways in the direction of the field house.

Almost everyone was wearing a button supporting one or another of the five candidates: GREG MONTGOMERY FOR PRESIDENT; VOTE FOR LAURA HOCH; ALL THE WAY WITH SETH WEINSTEIN; MICHELLE LINWOOD: THE RIGHT CHOICE. By far the most visible constituency, though, was the pro-Daniel crowd. In addition to buttons, they wore painter's caps and waved miniature banners on sticks.

Inside the field house, the scope of Daniel's campaign efforts was even more obvious. Lily craned her neck to see above the ocean of milling students. Each candidate had a space on the floor of the field house and a section in the bleachers marked by banners and signs. The Daniel Tackett signs were twice as big as anyone else's and much more professional. Not only that, but suspended from the field house ceiling was a net full of white balloons with multi-colored lettering: VOTE FOR DANIEL TACKETT, Lily read. She shook her head in admiration. She had to give Roxanne credit; she'd provided enough materials to get Daniel elected to the Senate!

Lily wandered from one candidate's camp to another, accepting a variety of handouts as she went. She really wasn't sure who to support. She wasn't feeling too kindly toward Greg after the way she was so ruthlessly snubbed at his headquarters the other day, but she wasn't ready to throw her loyalties back with Daniel and company, either. Maybe she'd support one of the other three students who were running. Undecided, she snagged a seat on the bleachers midway between Greg's faction and Daniel's, where she could see everything that was going on. She'd make up her mind democratically after hearing what each candidate had to say.

The five who were running had drawn lots to determine the order in which they would speak, with Greg drawing last and Daniel second to last. The first three speeches and demonstrations were relatively low-key and uneventful. It was already clear that even though the two final candidates hadn't been chosen yet, the only real contest was going to be between Greg and Daniel. By the time it was Daniel's turn to speak, the tension was starting to crackle, and when he approached the podium setup at one end of the temporary stage, bedlam broke loose. The demonstrations for the three previous candidates had been confined to some sign-waving and restrained cheering. But Daniel's supporters were rowdy, verging on out-of-control. The balloons had been dropped from the net and were being batted around incessantly. The chanting and cheering went on for a full five minutes before Daniel was able to wave the kids to partial silence so he could speak. And the chanting wasn't lighthearted or in fun. To Lily it sounded as if the theme of Daniel's demonstration was going to be "revolution."

Lily frowned as she peered down into the hullaballoo. She knew a lot of the pro-Daniel kids. Quite a few of them were former Stevenson friends and acquaintances. Even so, she wasn't sure she liked the way they kept shouting just to make noise. Just then she caught sight of an unmistakable redhead in a bright orange dress. It was Roxanne, tossing out yellow flyers and leading the chanting just like a cheerleader. Lily looked down at the pile of papers on her lap and pulled out a yellow sheet folded in thirds. The text inside was topped by a bold headline: PUT AN END TO MINORITY RULE! Lily read on: *Think about it. How well does the current student government represent your interests? If you're like the majority of Kennedy High students, your answer will be, "Not well at all." Daniel Tackett will change all that. Daniel Tackett will. . . .* Lily scanned the list of things Daniel planned to do, and then skipped down to the last sentence on the flyer: *It's time for a* REVOLUTION *in favor of* RESPONSIVE *student government. Be* RADICAL — *vote* DANIEL TACKETT FOR STUDENT BODY PRESIDENT.

Pretty heavy, Lily thought, refolding the handout and stuffing it and the others into the back pocket of her overalls. But not as heavy as it might be, considering Daniel's usual biting style. Roxanne had probably written it; she would know how to be forceful, but catchy, too.

When Daniel finally managed to break up the cheering and start talking, it was immediately apparent that his speech at least was all his own. He didn't use any flashy-sounding phrases. Instead he came right out and called everything as he saw it. "I haven't been at Kennedy very long," he began. "I transferred from Stevenson — " At the mention of Stevenson there were loud aggressive cheers from the pro-Daniel sections, punctuated by a few isolated boos. Daniel grinned and waved. "Like I said, I haven't been at Kennedy very long," he repeated, practically shouting into the mike. "But already I love it . . . and at the same time I hate it."

Lily leaned forward in her seat, her elbows propped on her knees and her eyes fixed on Daniel's dark, intense face. He talked fast but with precision. No one missed a word. And while he spoke, his gestures — a hand whipped through his longish brown hair, a finger stabbed in the air — lent a compelling urgency to his words. He was full of energy, but it was angry energy. As his speech progressed, the undercurrents in his words became more bitter and negative. "I love Kennedy. It's a big, strong school full of strong individuals," Daniel continued. "And I hate it because too many of those individuals are not fairly represented by the current student government. From all I've heard, that's been the case for a couple of years now. One elitist, self-perpetuating group has managed to get itself into power and stay there, leaving everybody else completely out in the cold. Now I won't mention any names, but you all know who I'm talking about."

Daniel's sarcastic, insinuating tone encouraged angry hisses from his supporters, which were countered by disparaging shouts from Greg's group. He grinned, clearly enjoying his power. "And it's obvious that the only way to turn things around here — change for the better's what we're all after, right? — is to toss that crowd right out of here. This election is your chance. You've been waiting for it!"

Even though Lily knew Daniel — and Roxanne and the rest of the Stevenson malcontents — too well to be swayed by his rhetoric, she couldn't help being just a little bit mesmerized by his magnetic presence. As she looked around, she saw she wasn't the only one who was affected. The expressions of a lot of kids, who a minute before had been yawning disinterestedly, were now rapt and animated. And Daniel didn't let their attention waver. His speech gained momentum as he continued to stress the unfairness of the current regime at Kennedy.

When his allotted time was up, Daniel left the podium promptly, but his supporters didn't take the cue. Or rather they *did* take the cue, Lily observed wryly to herself, only it was the cue from cheerleader Roxanne to keep yelling and hissing and shaking their signs and banners. Greg, meanwhile, had stepped up to the podium. He didn't attempt to speak into the microphone or even wave for quiet. There was no point. Daniel's demonstration was continuing unabated, and now Greg's supporters were getting in on the action and shouting right back.

Lily was frozen in her seat, waiting for the explosion. The scene looked to her sort of like a hockey game when a fight breaks out and the stands empty for a brawl. It didn't really matter at this point where the wildness had started — with Daniel's supporters or with Greg's — but fists were close to flying.

Just then Lily, who was half-searching for Jonathan while pretending to herself that she couldn't care less if she ever saw him again, caught a glimpse of his fedora in the fray. Her heart jumped and then nearly jerked to a halt when she thought she saw him duck a punch. After the way Jonathan had behaved toward her the other day she supposed he *did* deserve a sock in the eye, but even so, Lily couldn't bear to see a fight start. She sprang to her feet and began making her way down through the packed bleachers to the floor. She might not be sure whose side she was on, but she did know that this kind of feuding was all wrong. Maybe she could talk some of her old Stevenson friends into cooling it long enough for Greg to say his piece.

The noise on the floor was almost deafening

but suddenly, through the din of voices and the stomping of feet, Lily tuned into a couple of vaguely familiar voices nearby. She turned her head to the left. It was Frankie and her new boyfriend, Josh, the boy who did *Cloaks and Jokes*, which Lily enjoyed so much on WKND. Lily was surprised to hear that they were fighting — the last time she'd seen them together they couldn't seem to get close enough.

Josh had come up beside Frankie in passing and now he shouted at her. "Shouldn't you be wearing a Daniel Tackett button?"

Frankie, who had been focusing on the podium, whirled in Josh's direction. Her look of surprise changed to one of hurt and anger at his taunt. "What do you mean by that?" she shouted back, her raised voice barely audible in the middle of the crowded demonstration.

"Just that you're exactly like everybody else from Stevenson!" he accused, still yelling. "You're deceitful, untrustworthy . . . you're just as bad as Lily what's-her-name, with her made-up hard-luck story that Karen published and then, in good faith, sent to the journalism contest. Jonathan was finally smart enough to figure out how dishonest *she* really was. I guess it just took *me* a little longer to see through *you*!" Josh didn't give the dumbstruck Frankie time to catch her breath and respond. He stomped off, leaving Frankie near tears and Lily, standing a few feet off, in much the same condition.

"The made-up hard-luck story . . . the journalism contest . . ." Josh's words rang harshly inside

Lily's brain. What journalism contest? she wondered. Well, it really didn't matter. Lily hung her head, studying the toes of her worn sneakers. She had caused someone a lot of trouble. And she didn't even know it. All of a sudden she felt sick to her stomach. The noise and crush of people around her didn't help. Lily thought back to the day Daniel had dragged her into the newspaper office after talking her into playing a "joke" on Karen and the others. A joke, Lily had considered it, just for fun. A little bit of real-life acting. Sure Karen had printed the article in *The Red and the Gold*, but that was no big deal. A contest, though, would be completely different. In that case the same joke would become *fraud*.

No wonder Jonathan and all his friends despise me! she thought miserably. They had every reason to. They thought she was a liar, someone with no principles or respect for other people's feelings. Maybe *she* knew she wasn't that way, but she couldn't blame them — she couldn't blame Jonathan — for thinking so.

Lily raised her eyes and looked at Greg's demonstration and then toward the troublemakers grouped around Daniel's banners and signs. Troublemakers, that's all they are, she thought disgustedly. And troublemaking was what Daniel had been after with that interview, not fun. She realized she'd been used pretty thoroughly. The knowledge hurt her, upset her, and made her furious.

All of a sudden Lily didn't feel like talking to anyone. She retraced her steps to the bleachers and climbed back up to her seat. She might as well sit tight and hear what Greg had to say. She knew for sure she wouldn't vote for Daniel now if he were the last student alive.

Greg stood at the podium, looking down at the blur of excited faces with anxious eyes. He wasn't usually nervous speaking in front of a crowd. It was something he liked to do and he'd been pumped for it when the convention began. But by now what should have been an orderly, enjoyable event had deteriorated into a vicious free-for-all. Greg cleared his throat into the microphone, but it didn't have any effect on the shouting and catcalls. He considered just starting his speech whether anyone could hear him or not. For that matter, I might as well just walk off the stage, he thought, frustrated. No one would even notice.

Gripping the mike with one hand, Greg waved the other through the air. "Can I have your attention?" he shouted in his most authoritative tone. "Would you people please settle down?" Greg cringed inwardly. He sounded just like Principal Beman, and his words had probably only made matters worse. Looking at the crowd again, he saw he was right. Now, in addition to the harsh words being flung from one candidate's section to another, it looked like punches were flying, too.

Suddenly Greg's nervousness vanished, and he was just plain mad. It made him furious to see his school being turned into a battleground just because one small group of students was dissatisfied.

He was ready to curse out all the kids from Stevenson and maybe throw a few punches on his own, particularly if he could get his hands on Daniel Tackett.

His handsome face flushed, Greg leaned toward the mike, ready to lash out at Daniel and the accusations he'd made, give him a taste of his own medicine. Even as he opened his mouth to speak, though, he knew that anger wasn't the answer. Harsh, thoughtless words would only provoke the crowd more. He'd lose any chance he might still have of regaining control of the demonstration. And he knew he'd lose more than that. He'd lose the respect of his fellow students — and his own self-respect.

Greg closed his eyes for a second, trying to calm down so he could rationally decide what to do next. When he opened them and refocused on the action on the floor, he saw a beautiful, much-missed face beaming up at him. While all the students around her were talking or jumping or clapping or booing, Katie just stood still, a small island of peace and stability. She was carrying a huge VOTE FOR GREG MONTGOMERY sign that was almost as big as she was and smiling at him as if they were the only two people in the room. Greg stared down into her eyes, a smile touching his own face. What he saw there — strength, love, confidence — made him suddenly feel stronger. He didn't need to read Katie's lips to tell she was saying, "You can do it!" Yeah, he thought, I can. I've been in tough spots before. This is nothing!

He was already standing up straight, but now

Greg pulled his shoulders back to appear even taller than his six-feet two-inch frame. He brushed the sandy hair off his forehead and, with both hands in the front pockets of his khakis, he started talking. His voice was firm and commanding — he almost didn't need the assistance of the microphone. "I'm the last of the five candidates to go to bat today," he began, tearing his gaze away from Katie's to sweep the field house. "And the sooner you let me say a few words, the sooner we can all get out of here! I'd like a chance to share my thoughts with you as I hope you'll share your thoughts with me when — if — I become student body president."

It was an effort to make himself heard above the clamor, but he was succeeding, and as he took a breath before resuming, Greg thought the noise had lessened somewhat. This boosted his confidence even more. He started to reach for the cue cards tucked in his back pocket and then stopped. There were a couple things he wanted to say first that weren't part of his rehearsed speech. He glanced back at Katie. She waved her sign. Greg continued, "Before I talk specifics about what sort of things I'd like to see happen at Kennedy during my senior year, things that would make it a better school for us and for the kids who'll follow us here in the future, I want to tell you a couple of things I believe about being a student in general. About being caring, responsible, and involved."

Greg looked down and then back at his fellow students. "There've been a lot of opinions aired today and one of them in particular was pretty negative about the caliber of the students who've been involved as leaders at Kennedy this year." He was interrupted by a loud outburst of booing from Daniel's followers. He held up a hand. "It was a negative opinion," he insisted, "but no less valid because of that. What I believe, more than anything else, is that *anybody* who wants to play a part, to *really* 'make a change for the better' " — he quoted one of Daniel's campaign slogans — "should be allowed to do so. Anybody can get involved and be a leader. And there's no rule that says leadership has to be limited to the few people who are elected student body representatives. There are a lot of different kinds of talent and a lot of different ways to use it, and that's what this high school is all about."

Greg paused. The noise in the field house had died away to almost nothing. Most students were sitting down again, in the stands or on the floor. Only an occasional whistle or shout, or a low murmur of conversation competed with Greg's words now. "You know, it might take a lot of courage and imagination to challenge a system you think is unfair by suggesting it should just be torn apart, but I think it takes *more* courage and imagination to recognize what about that system works and to work to *improve* it, not simply destroy it," Greg declared emphatically. "I happen to think Kennedy has a pretty good student government, and the people who've been giving a lot of their time and energy to make things happen around here deserve some credit for that. I'll admit I've been pretty involved myself, and I plan to get *more* involved." He grinned and there was a rousing cheer from his supporters. "But the most important thing for us all to remember when it comes to choosing a new student body president, when it comes to anything in life, is to be *open.*" He paused again, allowing the words to resound forcefully throughout the field house. "We have to be open to new ideas and new participation. I believe everybody in this room has something to contribute to Kennedy High School. And I also believe a new student from Stevenson has as much to contribute as someone who's been at Kennedy for a couple years. I'm willing to open doors everywhere I can, but I just don't agree with anyone who says you have to slam some doors first. I don't think we need to tear anything down in order to make Kennedy High the best it can be."

By now the entire field house was silent. Greg had relaxed but the adrenaline was still flowing. Five minutes later, after reading from some of his notes, he finished his speech with as much power as he'd started. When he stepped away from the podium there was a pause, and then the crowd burst into spontaneous applause. Daniel's supporters cheered as boisterously as everyone else. Everything looked and sounded like normal again. The anger was gone.

Greg jumped down to the floor to receive the congratulations of his friends. "Hey, you were great! We've got it made!" Jonathan leaped into the air, thrusting a fist skyward.

"Thanks," Greg mumbled distractedly. He peered as best he could around Jonathan's flying limbs, searching for Katie. She was the one person he really wanted to see and to thank, but while the rest of the gang was hanging around to whoop it up, it looked like she had disappeared. Greg watched out for her for a full five minutes, until the field house was half empty, and then gave up. Katie hadn't stuck around. He almost began to wonder if he'd imagined her being there in the first place.

Greg listened with one ear to Jonathan's ideas on strategy for a final campaign push toward the election. Jonathan was assuming that after his strong showing at the convention Greg would be voted one of the two final candidates. Greg didn't bother trying to curb Jonathan's premature enthusiasm. He was still thinking about Katie showing up at his demonstration. It had been such an incredible, inspiring surprise. She'd really made the difference for him this afternoon, and not for the first time in his life.

Greg slipped away from his campaign team and out of the field house by a side door. He needed some time alone to think. As he went he found himself hoping it wouldn't be the last time, either.

Chapter 12

Lily swung her brown paper lunch bag as she walked toward the door in the south wing that led outside to the quad. On a day like this she guessed everyone would be eating outdoors — and she was right. The wooden benches were occupied and there were a dozen or more kids sitting on the grass. Frisbees were flying and WKND came in loud over the PA system. Lily took a deep breath of the balmy May air. What a perfect day! Too bad I have to spoil it by sitting with Roxanne, she thought with resignation. She didn't see anyone else she knew, though, or rather anyone else who'd tolerate her company. Elise, Adam, Jeremy, Diana, and Holly were clustered around the crowd's favorite bench under the far cherry tree, but joining them wasn't even an option these days. Lily would have to stick with the bench her Stevenson friends had claimed.

Roxanne was lying on her back on the grass with her head pillowed on her shoulderbag and the straps of her yellow tank dress pushed off her shoulders for better tanning. She looked up as Lily dropped her lunch bag on the ground next to her. "Don't you even *think* of sitting here until you take that atrocious button off your atrocious shirt!" she shrieked at Lily. Lily glanced down at her Grateful Dead T-shirt. She'd pinned a GREG MONTGOMERY FOR PRESIDENT button right through Jerry Garcia's nose. After the student assembly that morning, when it was announced that Greg and Daniel had been voted the two final candidates, Lily had dug the button out of her Kenya bag. She had also accumulated an assortment of Daniel items which she dumped back into her locker.

Lily met Roxanne's disdainful eyes squarely. "I'm endorsing Greg for president," she informed the group in a decided tone as she sat down. "Button or no button!"

"You're kidding!" Daniel, who was sitting with his back propped against the bench, snapped his head in Lily's direction. She couldn't see the expression in his eyes through his black Wayfarer sunglasses, but she figured it had to be as disbelieving as his voice.

"I kid you not," Lily assured him, pulling a peach out of her lunch bag and biting into it.

Daniel scowled. "In case you haven't noticed, he's running against *me*, as in my *opponent*. Where do you come off supporting him?"

Lily shrugged. "I went to the convention, I

read the handouts, I listened to the speeches, I chose a candidate. Pretty straightforward process, really."

Rox sat up so she could glare at Lily more effectively. "Traitor," she said accusingly.

A few of the others playfully echoed the sentiment. Zachary tried to make light of the situation by unpinning the Greg button from the front of Lily's shirt and refastening it on the back. "There, now Lily can advertise her political persuasion without offending us!" he declared with a grin.

Roxanne frowned at him. "This isn't a joke, Zack," she said irritably. "If Lily won't acknowledge the fact that Greg and his crowd don't want to have anything to do with anybody who transferred from Stevenson — no matter what he said in his goody-goody speech — then she shouldn't be hanging out here."

Lily threw down her peach, her eyes flashing with indignation. "If *I* won't acknowledge. . . ? What about all of you? You're the ones who won't admit the truth in all this." She fixed her eyes on Daniel and saw him flinch behind his dark glasses. "Frankly, I don't think Greg's the bad guy. And even if his speech was a bunch of bull, which it wasn't, what do you expect? That he and his friends should welcome us with open arms after we lied and hurt people? And don't look like you don't know what I'm talking about, any of you. Anybody from Kennedy who wasn't turned against Stevenson kids after the way Roxanne acted at the beginning of the semester *was* alienated when Daniel and I did that fake interview for the newspaper."

"But that was just a little practical joke," Daniel said, trying to calm Lily down.

"Oh, come off it!" Lily snapped. A strained note entered her voice. "I really can't believe you did that to me, Daniel. You know, you may not have realized it but you hurt me as much as you hurt Karen."

Lily stopped, biting her lip, her eyes filling dangerously with tears. Daniel looked genuinely taken aback and dismayed at the sudden quiver in Lily's chin. "I'm sorry," he said weakly.

Roxanne took this opportunity to charge back into the conversation. She was clearly smarting from Lily's accusations. "Daniel doesn't have anything to be sorry about," she informed Lily righteously. "And don't you dare insinuate that it was anything *I* did that turned that crowd against us. That's absolutely false and ridiculous. I *never* did anything to — "

"Spare me!" Lily was up in arms again. "You didn't do anything but make Frankie fix that computer Valentine service so you could get a hundred different dates." Roxanne looked innocent and shocked. "Don't act so outraged, Rox," Lily said. "Everybody knows that story by now. Were you really surprised when the guys stopped liking you?" She looked around at the glum expressions on the rest of the kids' faces. "Did you really have to take the rest of us down with you?"

Roxanne started to protest, but Lily didn't let her. Instead she whirled to face her again. "And what are we doing now?" she exclaimed. Rox cowered beneath her withering stare. "Just making ourselves look worse and worse by *still* following Roxanne, who we all know was the most ruthless person at Stevenson!"

Roxanne looked as if she wanted to retaliate, but for once the wind had been completely taken out of her sails. Lily paused, breathless from her outburst. Daniel pushed his sunglasses up on top of his head and opened and closed his mouth, red-faced. He was speechless, too. After a moment, he managed to recover enough to defend himself. He jerked his head and his glasses slipped off and bounced back down on his nose. "But Lily, Roxanne does have a point. They *have* excluded us. They . . . they wouldn't let me on the newspaper!" he sputtered.

"Did you ever ask," Lily insisted, "*before* you started getting revenge?"

Daniel didn't have an answer for this. For a brief moment Lily almost felt sorry for him. She'd known him for a long time. She knew how ambitious he was and understood how it must irk him to have been thwarted. And now he'd let Roxanne use him as the major pawn in her own elaborate game of revenge. But then Lily thought again about how she herself had been used, by people she considered her friends, and her sympathy waned.

Roxanne took advantage of the silence that followed Lily's question to regroup. "For once and for all, Lily, Daniel's doing the right thing," she said imperiously. Her diamond-studded watch glittered as she raised her hand to shake a finger at Lily. "He's taking a stand against an unfair system. That's the only way for anyone from

Stevenson to get what they deserve, what's fair."

Daniel nodded mechanically, but Lily shook her head. "No, no, no!" she exclaimed. "It's *not* the only way and it's not going to work." She ran her hand through her short blonde hair. "You're making a big mistake, Daniel," she warned him. "Just like I made a big mistake listening to you and Roxanne, and giving that fake interview in the first place. You've let her brainwash you, everybody, into thinking the Kennedy kids are all rats just because of her own personal grudge that they haven't crowned her queen bee like she was at Stevenson." Finished, Lily plunged a shaking hand into her lunch bag and pulled out a bag of homemade oatmeal raisin cookies. She offered one to Zack and bit into a second.

Talking to Roxanne and Daniel, trying to make them listen to themselves and how absurd their claims were, was like kicking a stone wall. She was getting bruised and exhausted just from the effort.

Roxanne took a strong sip from the straw stuck in her can of Tab. "You might as well go spout off your dumb opinions to some other audience," she advised Lily. "Daniel's running for president whether you like it or not. When he wins you'll change your tune."

Lily finished chewing the cookie and tucked the rest of them, along with her uneaten egg salad sandwich, back into her Kenya bag. Roxanne had thoroughly ruined her appetite. "Don't be so sure," she said as she got to her feet and brushed at the bits of grass clinging to her faded jeans. "From what I can tell, no one besides a few transfer students are going to vote for him. After Greg's speech, all the buttons and banners in the world couldn't buy Daniel enough votes."

"Don't be so sure of yourself, Lily Rorshack." Rox apparently had supreme confidence in the power of the publicity she'd orchestrated. "Daniel's committed to running, and his commitment is going to pay off, big time."

Lily sighed and stood for a moment, resting her weight on one foot. She studied Daniel's profile, willing back some of old respect and affection she'd felt for him. "Well, it's your life," she acknowledged, not even certain if he heard her. "If you want to follow Roxanne for the rest of your days, you can go ahead." She bent over to grab her bag and then, straightening up, turned to leave. "But count me out. I'm going to campaign for Greg whether you guys forgive me or not."

As Lily walked away from them, she knew she was probably taking an irrevocable step. Her old friends probably *wouldn't* forgive her for campaigning for Greg. Roxanne wouldn't, at least. She wasn't so sure about Daniel. As always, dark glasses or no dark glasses, he was a hard person to read. Lily looked around her, feeling a little bit like a boat that had broken loose from its mooring. It was a strange sensation to wander across the quad with no particular group to attach herself to. She realized she had cut herself off, maybe permanently, from her Stevenson roots without having put down new roots anywhere except perhaps in the Little Theater.

Lily thought briefly of Jonathan, and then forced his image from her mind. She couldn't count on him and his friends for stability. They had turned their backs on her the way she'd just turned her back on her Stevenson friends. Lily sighed deeply. Well, she would still campaign for Greg. No one could stop her from believing in him and what he stood for. Open doors . . . there had to be one for her out there somewhere.

Chapter 13

Friday was election day, and the day of the prom, too. The halls at Kennedy were even livelier than ever. Members of the junior and senior classes who'd volunteered to decorate the gym for the big night spent every spare minute there, transforming the big open space into a romantic garden of Eden. They put up streamers, bouquets of balloons, cut flowers, and even rented palm trees. In the main lobby, kids lined up to cast their votes for student body president in genuine voting booths with curtains and levers borrowed from the town hall. In the cafeteria, they lined up to purchase corsages and boutonnieres ordered from the Wilderness Club. Vince DiMase, president of the club, had temporarily become a florist in order to put some money into their treasury for summer outings.

After catching up with his old friend Vince for a little bit, Josh Ferguson grabbed a ham salad sandwich and then bolted for the radio station. He couldn't stand to watch all the prom-oriented goings-on knowing that he wouldn't be there with Frankie. He thought about the balloon he'd ordered a few weeks ago from the prom committee, a huge pink one with silver letters spelling out *Frankie and Josh*. The balloon would float on its ribbon all night, lonely and unclaimed. Not only that, there was a tuxedo reserved in his name at Rose Hill Formals that he hadn't had the heart to call and cancel. It would also sit, lonely and unclaimed. Kind of like me, Josh thought sadly. Then he gritted his teeth. There was no sense in feeling sorry for himself. At this point he considered himself as much to blame for the bad state of affairs with Frankie as she was. Maybe she'd started it by getting involved with Zachary, but he'd taken it from there.

Josh swung by the main lobby on his way to the station. He grimaced as he knocked on the vice-principal's door, remembering the confrontation with Frankie at the convention. He'd said some pretty nasty things to her, at the time believing they were just what she deserved. Now he pictured the hurt and surprise mingling with the anger on Frankie's pale, delicate face. Maybe I wasn't fair to her, he thought. Then he shrugged. It really didn't make any difference now.

At the conference table in Mrs. Goodwin's outer office, the freshman, sophomore, and junior class representatives were busy helping a secretary maintain a running total of the votes cast. Josh, who'd cast his own vote first thing that morning, jotted down the current totals so he could report it during his show, which was due to start in a couple of minutes.

Over at WKND, Brian was playing one last song while Karen waited to go to lunch with him. Josh waved for them to go ahead and then took his seat in the soundproof booth. It always gave him a funny kind of thrill, talking on the air. He planned someday to be a writer rather than a DJ, but he knew he'd miss the radio. He enjoyed telling stories out loud almost as much as putting them on paper. Now he wiped the palms of his hands on the knees of his blue-and-white seersucker pants, faded out the music, and launched into his own show.

First, the usual introductory remarks — *blah, blah, blah,* Josh thought. Then came campus news. His voice changed from mellow and chatty to purposeful and enthusiastic. "If you haven't voted yet, be sure to take a couple of seconds before the end of school to stop by the lobby and make your voice heard at Kennedy," he urged. "Everybody's doing it — so far fifty-one percent of the freshman, sophomore, and junior classes have turned out! And it's still a pretty close contest. Greg Montgomery's received four hundred and thirty-one of the votes cast with Daniel Tackett trailing — but not by much — with two hundred seventy-seven. Your vote *can* make a difference, so please don't forget."

Josh took a breath, pushed his glasses up on the bridge of his nose and rattled on. "Whoever gets elected will be meeting soon with the outgoing student body president, Colin Edwards, and the rest of this year's student government to talk over what's happened this year. Class elections will be held in September. Back to the here and now, though. There are still a couple of weeks left for things to happen at Kennedy before we all head off to summer fun and frolic. The spring teams are winding up their seasons and there've been some hot performances lately. Varsity baseball is undefeated — yes, un-de-feated. *And* they're on their way, I predict, to a shut-out in the division playoff against Leesburg. Boys' tennis was victorious yesterday against Maryville, and the gymnastics team squashed Carrolton Day School with Stacy Morrison pulling off a nine-point-five for first place in the floor excercise."

After a few more tidbits about sports and other extracurricular events, Josh knew it was time for a prom update. Suddenly it was a little bit harder to sound breezy. "The prom's tonight, in case anybody forgot," he announced, surprised by the wistful note in his voice. He hoped the whole school couldn't hear it. "You can buy tickets in the cafeteria today or at the door tonight. And if you're not going because you don't have a date," Josh said, wincing. "Go anyway. And then again, there's always next year. If you're a senior, there might not be a prom to look forward to, but there'll be something around the corner that's just as good. So . . . what else can we talk about? I know, summer jobs. Yeah, once you're sixteen, summer just doesn't mean the beach, the pool, the tennis courts, the lawn mower. If you're looking for work, drop by the career counseling office and check out the list of local stores and camps that are hiring summer help. As for me, I wish I could be spending the summer in Raspberry Patch, but it looks like I'll be passing most of the daylight hours at Ferguson's Hardware Store, the place for all your home and garden needs. But hey, don't think time's going to stand still in Raspberry Patch while all of us are on vacation!" He paused, improvising. "The soda fountain'll still be open for business and the Raspberry Patchers will be stopping in more often than usual 'cause of the thirsty summer weather. A few things have changed there, though, along with the seasons. That guy who's been the most regular customer at the fountain all spring won't be going there anymore. He's spent so many hours hanging over the counter staring at the girl who scoops the ice cream, they should retire his stool! No, he didn't lose his taste for ice cream or for the soda-fountain girl. But he got kind of caught up in trying to impress her, pretending to be a fireman or the sheriff or a — " Josh gulped. "Or a football hero. Then he realized the best person to be was himself. It took some guts, and it meant giving up his dreams of the soda-fountain girl, but he did it. Anybody can do it, can be himself or herself. Take it from me. So next time you look in the mirror, if the face there isn't yours, gather up your courage and put the original back where it belongs."

Josh ended his daily story with a slight pang. He always put a lot of himself into the Raspberry Patch fables, but usually not *that* much. Still, he didn't suppose anyone would recognize the characters, except — he felt another stab somewhere around the general vicinity of his heart — except maybe Frankie.

"Speaking of being yourself," he said quickly, realizing he'd fallen into silence, the cardinal sin of radio broadcasting, "here's a classic on that subject." He put on a record Brian had left lying around, "Born to be Wild." Not exactly my style, Josh thought wryly as the music began. But it was better than nothing. Slipping down from the stool he left the booth to rummage through the record closet, pulling five records out at random. Back in the booth, he set them to play one after another. He needed to take five, get his head back together.

After closing the door to the booth behind him, Josh threw himself down on the office's overstuffed armchair. Tipping his head back, he shut his eyes and took a couple of deep breaths.

Raspberry Patch, U.S.A. Sometimes he really did wish he lived there. Things always worked out smoothly, lessons were learned without too much trauma.

Real life, on the other hand . . . Josh rubbed his eyes and frowned. A week ago he would have been sneaking over to the gym to rush through a Nautilus routine. He laughed out loud with genuine amusement. As if all the sit-ups and push-ups in the world could have made him look like Zack McGraw! Yeah, he'd learned his lesson the hard way, with lots of sore muscles and a very sore — most likely broken — heart. Greg's speech the other day had said a lot to Josh, personally as well as politically. He thought about how wrong and ridiculous it was to try and be something you weren't, how the best thing you could do for yourself and for the people around you, for the whole world even, was to make the most of your own unique gifts and talents.

So that was what Josh had decided to do. Maybe he wasn't a jock but, instead, just an unathletic storyteller with glasses and no date for the prom. He could — he would! — accept and be happy with that.

Then why, he wondered, opening his eyes to stare blankly at the torn U2 poster on the opposite wall, do I feel sort of like crying or beating my head against the wall or something? And why do I keep missing Frankie *so much*?

"Who did *you* vote for, Katie?" Molly asked slyly. The two were lounging on the quad during lunch, soaking up the sun and listening to WKND. Frankie had just joined them with her own lunch.

Katie, who was lying on her back, didn't bother to open her eyes but simply smiled at Molly's tone. "I guess I'm one of the four hundred and thirty-one — so far," she said, hedging.

"Who. . . ?" Molly prompted.

"Greg," Katie admitted with a laugh. "Want to make something of it?"

Molly was propped up on her elbows so she could study her best friend's expression. Now she flopped backward on the grass. "Not really," she said amiably. "Just checking."

"What about you, Frankie?" It was Katie's turn to ask. "It must be a hard choice, with Daniel being your old Stevenson classmate and all."

Frankie blushed slightly, recalling Josh's insults

at the convention. "Actually, it wasn't," she told Katie. "I've been supporting Greg's candidacy from the beginning, remember?"

"Oh, that's right." Katie sounded vague, and it occurred to Frankie that the other girl might be a little embarrassed at acknowledging the fact that she hadn't played much of a part in her ex-boyfriend's campaign.

She was about to change the subject away from the election when Molly did it for her. "So, are you and Josh all set for the prom, Frankie?" Molly asked, swatting at a fly on her tanned forearm.

Frankie blushed again. "Um, uh. . . ." She hadn't told anyone, not even her family, about her fight with Josh. She'd kept hoping that she'd have a chance to explain things to him, but after their run-in at the convention, it was starting to look as if they might never speak to one another again. Half of Frankie wanted to confide in Katie and Molly right now, get their sympathy and advice. But the other half wasn't sure she was ready for sympathy and advice quite yet. She had a feeling it might just make her cry. "Yeah, pretty much," she lied in answer to Molly's question. "What about you guys?"

Molly beamed. "Ted's coming home from James Madison for the weekend!" she said brightly. Her boyfriend, Ted Mason, was a freshman at the Virginia college. "Even though he has final exams next week, he says the senior prom is too important to miss." She looked at her watch and her smile grew even wider. "I'm meeting him at the train station in only five hours!" Then she glimpsed Katie's sad face and her own face fell. "Whoops! K.C., I'm sorry. I didn't mean to rub it in," she said.

Katie rolled over on her stomach and pillowed her face on her arms. She managed a weak smile. "That's okay, Moll," she assured her friend. "I'm glad Ted'll be here — you guys are going to have a great time! I'll be thinking about you."

"We'll be thinking about *you.*" Molly leaned over to give Katie's shoulder a squeeze. "And don't you forget it! Besides" — she smiled mischievously — "it's not as if you didn't get asked. You could be going to the prom if you wanted to."

"With who?" Frankie wondered, curiously.

Katie laughed. "Eric," she said, naming her former boyfriend. "For old times' sake, I guess. We've ended up being good friends, but somehow going to the senior prom together . . . it wouldn't have felt right. There's only one person. . . ." She shook her head, obviously trying to clear it of any thoughts of Greg. "Instead, I fixed Eric up with a girl on the gymnastics team," she finished lightly. "Stacy Morrison."

The three girls sunbathed in silence for a few minutes. Frankie toyed with a blade of grass between her fingers, trying to ignore the WKND broadcast. Listening to Josh's sweet, familiar voice reeling off the latest Kennedy sports statistics was like having salt rubbed in her wound. Katie was brave enough to share the details of her datelessness, she reasoned. Suddenly the half of Frankie that wanted to talk won out. "You guys," she began abruptly. "I lied when I said Josh and I were all set for the prom. We're not all set, in fact, we're not even going!"

"What?" Molly exclaimed. Katie sat up, a look of concerned surprise on her sun-flushed face.

Frankie had to bite back tears as she told the whole story to Katie and Molly, starting with the scene at the track with Zachary and finishing with the shouting match during the convention.

The other girls were outraged and understanding. "That's terrible!" Molly declared while Katie leaned forward to give Frankie a reassuring hug.

Frankie sniffled her agreement. "It really is. Oh, I just wish I could go back to that day before I let Zack kiss me! I mean, it wasn't his fault. But I really didn't mean for anything like that to happen."

"Have you tried explaining that to Josh?" asked Katie reasonably.

Frankie shrugged sadly. "I haven't had a chance to. How can I explain anything to him when he's determined to believe the worst of me?"

Katie pondered this thoughtfully. Then her auburn eyebrows curved in a questioning frown. "But Frankie, didn't you — sorry to be nosy and all that — but didn't you used to have a crush on Zachary? A pretty bad one?"

"Yeah, but that's past history," Frankie protested. "I haven't felt anything for Zack since I met Josh. Josh is the only guy I care about!"

"Maybe *that's* what you should tell him," Molly suggested, pushing the sleeves of her royal-blue T-shirt up over her elbows. "He might not have known about your old crush, but maybe he sensed it somehow. Maybe he thinks you've liked Zack better than him all along. You've got to tell him that's not true."

Frankie bent her head to study her unpolished toenails. "I want to," she admitted. "I just don't know how — or where — or when."

They all thought about this problem, and just then Josh, having wrapped up the school news on the radio, faded in to his Raspberry Patch, U.S.A., episode. Frankie listened carefully, not wanting to miss a single nuance. And the story, or at least the side she was hearing now for the first time — Josh's side — was straightforward. Is that what he thinks I want? She was astonished. A football hero? Did he honestly think I didn't want him, didn't adore him, just the way he was?

His story over, Josh set "Born to be Wild" blasting. Katie hugged her knees and looked at Frankie intently. "That was Josh, huh?" she said. "It sounds like he was talking about you."

Frankie nodded. "I think he was."

"So, you said you weren't sure how or where or when to try and talk to him." Katie smiled encouragingly. "Well, how about now, at the radio station!"

Frankie had been thinking the same thing, but she was frozen with indecision. "But what should I say?" she pleaded.

Katie shook her head helplessly. "You know better than us what Josh needs to hear."

Frankie took a deep, shaky breath. "You're right. I'll go over there this minute. Before I chicken out." She scrambled to her feet. Once she'd made a decision, she couldn't slow down. "Thanks, guys!" she called back to them as she headed across the quad at a trot.

"Good luck!" Molly and Katie cheered in spirited voices.

Frankie didn't stop running until she'd reached the familiar WKND door. Then she hesitated, breathless. What on earth *was* she going to say to Josh? Somehow "I'm sorry" didn't seem good enough. For about the millionth time, Frankie wished she had Josh's way with words. She wished she could turn her thoughts and feelings into stories as easily as he could. Well, maybe I can, she thought with sudden courage. I can try, anyway!

She knocked on the door, but so lightly that Josh couldn't possibly have heard her. When she eased the door open, she saw him sitting with his eyes squeezed shut. They popped open at the click of the door closing behind her. To say he looked slightly surprised would have been like saying Frankie looked slightly nervous.

Josh had been slouched in the chair, but suddenly he drew himself up straight. The vulnerable expression that had been in his eyes a moment before was quickly replaced by a guarded one. He nodded at Frankie to acknowledge her presence. "What . . . what are you doing here?" he asked, the crack in his voice belying his cool tone.

Frankie felt awkward standing while Josh was sitting but there was no other chair nearby so, ignoring her white linen pants, she dropped onto the dusty linoleum floor to sit cross-legged, facing Josh.

"I — I wanted to tell you something," she explained shyly. "I heard your show." She gestured at the broadcast booth and Josh flushed. "And I wanted to tell you I — she. . . ." Frankie faltered and then she knew exactly how to tell her story. "The soda-fountain girl — she's been kind of lonely lately. Scooping ice cream just isn't as much fun as it used to be." Josh raised his eyebrows and Frankie continued. "You know, she never really liked the football hero all that much. I mean, she didn't really know him very well. It was just when he leaned over the counter and kissed her she didn't know what to do! It's the other boy she cares about, and misses, and loves. And she was wondering, will he ever soften up and drop by the soda fountain to sit on his old stool again?"

By now Frankie's cheeks were pinker than Josh's. She dropped her eyes, embarrassed. She felt helpless. She'd said her lines and now it was up to Josh.

He put his hands on the arms of the chair and leaned forward eagerly. "Do you really mean that?" he asked, his voice husky.

Frankie raised her eyes to his. They were sparkling with hopeful tears. "Yeah, I do," she answered softly.

Josh lunged forward off the chair to give Frankie a hug just as she jumped to her feet to do the same. They bumped heads and then tumbled back onto the chair in a giddy tangle.

"You mean the soda-fountain girl's not going to the prom with the jock?" Josh asked incredulously.

Frankie rubbed her nose against his. "Nope. In

fact, the soda-fountain girl has a brand-new dress hanging in her closet. She bought it before this crazy misunderstanding happened, and she doesn't want to wear it for anyone but you."

Josh grinned. "Wahoo!" he hollered, mussing Frankie's already tousled hair with one hand. Then his smile faded slightly and behind his glasses, his eyes clouded over. "But you and Zachary, you. . . ."

Frankie shook her head firmly." There's nothing between us," she reassured him. "Unless of course he buys my tutoring services at another auction!" When Josh still looked doubtful, she became serious again. "It's true I used to have a thing for him. The soda-fountain girl *did* have a hopeless crush on the football hero. But that was before she met you and found out what love was really all about."

Josh put a hand to his glasses self-consciously. "I'm not as good-looking as he is, though. Or as athletic and muscular and — "

Frankie put her hand over his mouth. "Don't talk yourself down like that!" she exclaimed. "None of that stuff is important, and besides, *I* think you're extremely cute! Josh, remember when we first met and I wouldn't listen to you when you said nice things to me and told me you thought I was beautiful? I was so used to thinking of myself as Roxanne's shadow that I couldn't see what *I* had to give. I could never compete with her. But you helped me believe I was special." She smiled at him, her heart in her eyes. "Now it's my turn. I think *you're* special. Do you believe me?"

In answer, Josh pulled her close and kissed her.

They held each other tight for a long moment, neither one wanting to let go. They'd come so close to losing each other that it would be a while before they could take even the smallest kiss or hug for granted.

Suddenly Josh scrambled out of the chair, bouncing Frankie off his lap. The last of the records he'd put on had just ended. "Quick, Frankie! Grab an album!" he shouted, dashing into the booth.

Without even looking where she was reaching Frankie whipped a record off the shelf and practically threw it at Josh. He glanced at the song title and grinned, saying into the microphone, "Here's one for all you prom-bound lovers out there. Have a grand evening! 'I Only Want To Be With You.' "

Josh held Frankie's eyes through the booth's window, still smiling. She smiled back. "Me, too," she whispered.

Chapter 14

"The next President of the Kennedy High School Student Body will be Gregory Montgomery!" The loudspeaker announcement came at the end of last period and was greeted by cheers, applause, whistles, and handshakes. Everyone active in the campaign had been excused from class and Greg's headquarters was packed with people all trying to congratulate him at once.

"Way to go, Monty!" Matt yelled, throwing his Baltimore Orioles cap in the air.

"Yay, Greg!" Molly stretched up on tiptoes to give him a victory kiss.

"All right!" Eric roared enthusiastically.

Jonathan managed to make his way to Greg's side. He gave his friend an enormous grin. "You did it!" he exclaimed, clapping him on the shoulder.

"*We* did it," Greg corrected, grinning back. "It was a team effort."

When the last-period bell rang a moment later, the crowd began to disperse. They were planning to celebrate the victory properly that evening at a post-prom party at Diana's. Even though Greg wasn't going to the dance, he'd promised to stop by so they could make a fuss over him.

Karen stayed behind, joining Greg and Jonathan where they were standing. "I know you guys want to get out of here and get a head start celebrating." She looked at her watch and smiled. "I want to go home and start getting ready for the prom! But what about staying for just a few minutes to work on your acceptance speech?"

Greg grimaced. "But I don't have to make it until assembly on Tuesday," he pointed out.

"Yeah, but if you get some of it on paper now I can include excerpts from it in the newspaper, which is going to the printer on Monday so it can be distributed Wednesday," Karen said reasonably.

Greg looked cornered. Jonathan laughed. "You can't argue with the woman," he said pushing Greg firmly down in the chair behind the desk. "She's a reporter!"

Jonathan pulled up another chair and Karen perched on the desk and all three set to work composing a victory speech. Greg would scribble a sentence or half a paragraph and read it out loud, then Jonathan and Karen would either nod their approval or recommend changes. They were so preoccupied with this project that they didn't hear the door open. When they finally looked up, Daniel Tackett was walking toward them.

Greg, for whom being a good sport whether he

won or lost was one of the most important doctrines of his life, stood up and held out his hand to shake Daniel's. Jonathan and Karen stayed seated, suspicious expressions darkening both their faces. Daniel's usually aggressive, defensive look was absent. Instead his hesitant smile was friendly, even humble. "Greg," he began, taking Greg's outstretched hand briefly and then pushing his fists deep into the pockets of his faded black jeans. "I wanted to congratulate you. I think you'll be an excellent president," he said sincerely.

"Thanks." Greg shrugged, playing his victory down with an offhand smile. "You mounted a strong campaign. It was pretty close all the way to the wire."

"Not really." There was no trace of bitterness in Daniel's voice. "You deserved to win and it's a credit to the students at Kennedy, including the transfers, that they recognized that."

Greg accepted this statement with a gracious nod. Jonathan merely raised his eyebrows. Karen, however, couldn't quite manage to keep from humphing under her breath.

To her surprise, Daniel now turned in her direction. "Karen, you're really the one I was looking for. I'd like to apologize," he said, his gaze direct, "for pulling that prank on you with the article about Lily."

Karen wasn't as easygoing and forgive-and-forget as Greg. "Oh?" Her voice was cool.

Daniel ran a hand nervously through his hair. "I'd like you to know that the whole thing was my idea," he continued. "Not that I think it's anything to brag about," he assured her. "I'm pretty ashamed of the way I acted. But Lily . . . she didn't really know what was going on. She thought it was just a joke, and she certainly didn't know about the contest. But I did, and I have no excuse for not speaking up when you submitted the article."

The three were stunned by Daniel's speech. When Karen responded, her attitude wasn't as hard-edged as it had been a moment before. "Well, thanks for setting us straight," she said, with an uncertain look at Greg and Jonathan. "But if you don't mind my asking, why didn't you? Speak up, I mean."

Daniel hung his head, his eyes hidden behind an unruly shock of dark hair. He kicked the toe of his right sneaker against the floor. "Closed-mindedness, I guess," he answered finally. "It's probably no secret to any of you that feelings between your crowd and mine have been a little sour. I've got to admit that most of the animosity has come from us. We really jumped to conclusions — we thought you guys didn't want any part of us. I was already convinced of that the day I stopped by the newspaper office. Well, I think I know better now. Your speech" — he nodded at Greg — "made it pretty clear that *me* accusing *you* of not being open and fair was way out of line." He attempted a smile, shifting his weight uncomfortably. "So, I'm sorry, Karen. I guess you've just got to take my word for it."

Karen hopped down from the desk so she could step closer to Daniel and look him right in the eye. "Thanks," she said simply. Her expression was still reserved but now it was glad, too. "Thanks for clearing things up." She appeared to think something over for a moment and then arrived at a decision, adding "You know, we can always use good people on the newspaper. I was really impressed with *The Stevenson Sentinel* you gave me that time. Would you like to join the staff of *The Red and the Gold*? I know the school year's almost over, but there's still time to get a couple of issues under your belt before next year's editors are elected."

Daniel's face lit up. "That'd be fantastic!" He accepted her offer without hesitation, grateful and pleased. "I'd really like to have a chance to work with you." His mouth twisted in a mischievous smile. "I've really come to respect *The Red and the Gold*, and I hate to admit it but I think it's even a better rag than the old *Sentinel*."

Karen tossed her wavy black hair and laughed. "Well, I'll admit *I* got some ideas from that issue of *The Sentinel* you showed me. In fact, I'd like to see you doing something new for *The Red and the Gold*. The position I envision — and you'd be perfect for it! — would be a sort of roving editor, an editor-at-large, however you want to call it." Karen assumed a businesslike stance, with her hands on her hips. "Someone who'd go outside of Kennedy for stories, to the national level if you thought it was appropriate, but who'd also tap the students for opinions. . . ."

Karen and Daniel plunged into an animated conversation about this and other editorial possibilities. Greg joined in, clearly feeling his new responsibility as student body president and wanting to know everything that was going on. Jonathan, meanwhile, couldn't have risen from his chair if he'd wanted to. He stared into space, his mouth hanging open. Karen, Greg, Daniel, Greg's victory, and Greg's victory speech were all forgotten. "Lily didn't know what was going on . . . about the contest. The whole thing was my idea. . . ." Daniel's words galloped around Jonathan's brain, deafening him to anything else. Lily didn't know! he thought, dumbfounded. She was innocent! Well, maybe not *innocent*, but at least not as guilty as he'd thought. And he'd been so mean to her! Jonathan remembered the look on Lily's face that afternoon she'd stopped by Greg's campaign headquarters to volunteer to help. He thought of how he'd totally, cruelly, blown her off. He could have kicked himself.

He looked down at his hands and saw that he was mechanically squashing his fedora. Why hadn't he given Lily the benefit of the doubt? Or at least confronted her? He'd been so unfair to believe his friends and not Lily without knowing her half of the story. Especially since he was crazy about her. Maybe it was because of those feelings that he'd acted like such an idiot. He was afraid of being hurt again, having a girl he cared about make him look like a fool. Well, he'd succeeded in making a pretty thorough fool out of himself without Lily's help. So *now* what? How could he apologize to her when she probably never wanted to speak to him again?

Jonathan decided he could only try. If she slammed the door in his face and he had to apologize to the welcome mat, at least he would have given it a shot. He hadn't stopped thinking about Lily for a minute, even after he'd learned about her supposed role in the feud. He'd been as wild about her as before. Only now it hurt because he thought he'd never share another goofy conversation with her, or another steamy kiss in the cab of her truck. She was worth it — those memories were worth it. He had to try.

Jonathan sprang to his feet and leaped for the door, clutching his fedora. Greg, Karen, and Daniel were nearly bowled over. They stared after him, astonished, but Jonathan didn't slow down to explain. He sprinted through the halls and out to the parking lot, and even climbed in his car and started the engine before he realized he didn't even know where Lily lived — all he knew was her phone number. He practically fell out of Big Pink and then sprinted back to the lobby. The pay phone there wasn't being used, which was fortunate because Jonathan might have committed an act of violence to get his hands on the directory, which was attached to the phone booth by a rattly chain. Grabbing the book, he fumbled through it, ripping pages out left and right in his haste. *Rorshack, Rorshack, Rorshack* . . .There it was — he recognized the number he had dialed several times before. And there was only one Rorshack in the whole town of Carrolton, Maryland.

On the way back out to his car, Jonathan repeated the address in his head so he wouldn't forget it. *67 Sassafras Street*. Where exactly was that? He hoped it would be right off the town's main drag, and as he left the fringes of Rose Hill and drove through Carrolton's center, he discovered he was right. Sassafras Street was a left past the bakery at the fourth set of lights. The numbers were going backwards — 377, 371, 369 — and the houses and lots got a little bigger the farther out from town he went. Jonathan thought he would never get there, but in just a few minutes he was pulling his car over alongside the curb by a pretty white clapboard house with green shutters and an enormous willow tree in the front yard.

He cut the engine and sat in the car for a minute. Suddenly he'd run out of steam. What was he doing there, anyway? He didn't know Lily that well. He couldn't even guess how she'd take this visit. Would she be happy? Furious? Amused? Disinterested? All of the above? There was only one way to find out.

Jonathan eased out of Big Pink, accidentally slamming the door very loudly behind him. Great, he thought, everybody in the neighborhood probably heard that! They were all probably looking out their windows right now. "Who's that idiot in the hat going into the Rorshacks' driveway? Probably another one of that wild Lily's weird boyfriends." Did Lily have a lot of boyfriends, weird or otherwise? Jonathan now found himself wondering. Maybe she'd already forgotten all about him. Maybe she'd found another date to the prom. He looked up as he neared the top of the driveway. There was a rusted basketball hoop over the garage doors. Lily probably had a very tall brother who had heard how Jonathan and his friends had tarnished his sister's reputation. Jonathan shook his head briskly. There was no point in imagining all the possible scenarios. There was no time. He was on the Rorshacks' front steps pressing the doorbell.

Jonathan gulped as someone unlatched the door from the inside, ready for the imaginary brother or maybe even Lily's father with a sawed-off shotgun. Instead it was Lily herself. She peered out at him through the screen door, her big eyes as round as full moons under the blonde wisps of her bangs. Lily didn't turn around and leave like Jonathan was afraid she would. She just stood there staring out at him wordlessly.

Jonathan shuffled his feet. "Um, can I, uh, come in?"

Lily came back to life. "Sure! Of course. Sorry, I just wasn't expecting you." She opened the door and Jonathan stepped into the hall.

"Were you expecting someone else?" he asked, fearing the worst.

"No," she said. "Just not *you.*"

They stood in the hallway for a moment looking at one another cautiously. Lily, in flowered boxer shorts, was balancing on one bare foot, the other tucked up behind her knee. Jonathan thought she had never looked cuter or more appealing. He also thought she'd never looked more mysterious. He couldn't read her expression any better than if she'd had her mime's makeup on.

Lily realized she was doing it again. "Sorry, I keep making you just stand there! Want to sit down?"

"Yeah," Jonathan said eagerly. He followed Lily down the hall and through a big, open country kitchen. A marmalade cat startled him by jumping off the top of the refrigerator as he walked by, practically sending him through the ceiling. Lily pushed open French doors leading onto a sunny back porch. She pointed to an old-fashioned wooden swing. "Is this okay?"

Jonathan would have been happy to sit on the floor. "Just fine," he assured her.

They sat down side by side on the swing. Jonathan took off his hat and rested it on his knees. He felt like he was courting Lily in some old western movie or something.

"So?" The syllable jolted Jonathan out of his fogged state. He turned to look at Lily and she looked back at him calmly.

"So?" she repeated.

"So . . . what?" Jonathan said, puzzled.

"So, what are you doing here?"

"I came to talk to you," Jonathan answered.

Lily laughed. "I didn't think you came to sell Girl Scout cookies!" He laughed, too, and Lily waited for him to start. When he didn't she pressed him again. "Why do you want to talk to me?" Her smile faded and her mouth set in bitter lines. "It didn't seem like you had much to say to me the last time we saw each other."

Jonathan wrinkled his eyebrows with regret and dismay. "I'm sorry, Lily. I'm sorry," he said urgently. "I know I hurt your feelings and I hate myself for it."

Lily turned her face away to pick at a small piece of paint peeling off the arm of the swing. "Then why'd you do it?" she asked quietly.

Jonathan knew he had to be honest. "Because my friends told me about the fake interview you and Daniel did for Karen and how much trouble it almost got her in. I hadn't even heard the story before. I must have been in outer space or something. Anyway, when I heard about that and with the feud and all, it looked like . . . you weren't what you seemed to be."

"You thought I was a liar." Lily made it a statement not a question.

Jonathan hung his head. "Yeah, I did. But even though I knew we were supposed to be on opposite sides, I couldn't help still thinking about you all the time. Like Romeo and Juliet. I'm sorry."

He expected Lily to get mad or cry, but instead she just shrugged her thin shoulders and sighed. "I guess I really can't blame you," she admitted. "I must have looked pretty bad."

"But not anymore!" Jonathan said in a rush. "That's why I came over! Daniel apologized to Karen — I was there, too — and said you hadn't even known about the journalism contest!"

Lily raised one fine eyebrow. "Oh, so now it's okay to be associated with me again?"

"That's not what I meant," he protested. He looked in vain for a teasing sparkle in Lily's eyes. "Well, maybe that's a tiny part of it. But the big part of it is that I realized I'd been really unfair to you. I came over to see if I could make it up to you. If maybe we could . . . if we could try again."

Lily considered this. "I don't know." She still looked offended, and Jonathan wasn't sure if she were pretending or not. "You were too uptight to believe in me before. Are you sure you want to let down your guard? What if this truce between our crowds is a false alarm? I mean, look what happened to Romeo and Juliet!" Lily pretended to play a violin and hummed the music from the movie.

Now the teasing sparkle was there. Jonathan grabbed Lily to give her a bear hug. She giggled. "Okay, go ahead and give me a hard time," he told her. "I deserve it! I was a jerk."

Lily wriggled out from his grasp and crossed her arms over her chest. She gazed up at him with a straight face. Then she scowled. "Lily Rorshack, huh?" she growled in a deep voice. "One of those bad-news kids from Stevenson. Not surprised to hear it. Knew it all along. From the first time she tried to steal my hat!"

Jonathan's anxious look dissolved and he burst out laughing. This time when he grabbed Lily she didn't wriggle away. They lay in one another's arms laughing so hard the swing started rocking wildly, threatening to spill them out onto the porch floor. After a moment, they both caught their breath and the swing slowed. Jonathan gazed down into Lily's upturned face. "So, are we on for the prom?"

Lily had forgotten all about the prom. She wiped a tear of laughter from her eyes and beamed, delighted. "You bet!"

Jonathan was leaning over about to give her a kiss on her smiling lips when her expression changed dramatically. "What's the matter?" he asked, worried.

"What are we going to *wear*?" Lily exclaimed. "The prom's tonight and I hadn't found a dress before you disinvited me!"

Her panic was contagious. Jonathan groaned. "And you can bet there's not a single rental tux left in the whole county!"

They pondered their dilemma, the swing jerking in time to the frantic tapping of Jonathan's foot. Then Lily's puckered frown cleared. She grinned mischievously at Jonathan. "I've got an idea." She gripped his hand and pulled him to his feet. "Come on!"

Jonathan broke into a trot to keep up with her as she dashed through the house, out the front door, and down the driveway, not even bothering to stop to put on some shoes. She stopped in front of Big Pink. "We'll have to take your car. My dad has the truck," she apologized breathlessly.

"Where are we going?" He started the engine and turned around in the Rorshacks' driveway.

"You'll see!" She wouldn't say anything else except to direct him "right," "left," or "straight at the stop sign." In a few minutes, though, Jonathan realized they were heading back to school.

"What . . . ?" he wondered as she steered him into the Kennedy parking lot. Then he grinned. "Not the costume room at the Little Theater!"

"Yep!" She laughed as they crossed the parking lot hand in hand, the warm breeze blowing her hair over her face. "I hope we can find something!"

After the bright sunlight, the dimness backstage was almost impenetrable. Lily and Jonathan felt their way down the cluttered hallway until they came to the costume storage area. He fumbled for the light switch. The odd exotic costumes seemed to fill out in the flickering light, take on lives of their own.

Jonathan began by sorting through a box of men's formal trousers while Lily rustled among the dresses. "Ugh!" she finally exclaimed, turning her back on the rack in disgust. "These would all make me look like Queen Elizabeth . . . the *First*," she added grimly. She bypassed another rack of dresses after announcing that the 1920s flapper style really wasn't her, either. Then she joined Jonathan just as he pulled a pair of dark emerald tuxedo pants with a satin stripe down the side out of the box. "Those would be perfect on me!" she declared, gleefully snatching them from him.

"Wait, I was going to wear them." Jonathan grabbed them back. "You'd look better in a dress, anyhow."

"No, I want to wear trousers," she said stubbornly. "Besides, they look too small for you."

"*Au contraire*," Jonathan argued. "They look too *big* for *you!*"

"They're not your color." Lily sounded certain of this. "They'd be much better on me!" She tugged on the pants, glaring.

"But I found them first!" Jonathan tugged — and glared back. Then they both broke into peals of laughter. The pants fell back into the box, forgotten, as Lily fell into Jonathan's arms. "Familiar scene, huh?" he asked, nuzzling her neck. Everything else in the room smelled like mothballs, but Lily smelled like lilacs.

"It's like meeting for the first time all over again," she agreed. Then her lips curved into a sly smile. "Better, actually. That first time you didn't know me well enough to kiss me."

Jonathan smiled, too, as he brought his face close to hers. "But now I do," he said huskily. "And I'm going to!" They kissed, tumbling happily backward into a pile of old clothing. They were on for the prom — and maybe a whole lot more.

Chapter 15

Katie tooted the horn of her mom's Plymouth Voyager as she pulled out of Molly's driveway. Turning her head, she could see Molly waving at her from her living room window. She smiled and faced forward again, braking for a stop sign with a sigh. It had been fun watching Molly get dressed for the prom and helping her with her hair and her makeup, but not *that* fun. Not as fun as it would have been to be doing all that herself. Instead, here she was in Bermuda shorts and an oversized T-shirt, heading for the sub shop to indulge in a solitary mocha milk shake. What a prom night, she thought with an even deeper sigh.

She stuck her arm out of the car window as she cruised down the big hill on Main Street that flattened out into downtown Rose Hill. The wind whipped her hair wildly. Below her, the town was bathed in the golden light of a spectacular spring sunset. It was going to be a beautiful night: balmy, fragrant, star-filled . . . perfect for a prom, Katie observed wistfully to herself. Then she had to laugh. There was just no way to escape it. She wasn't at the prom so she'd probably spend the whole night thinking about it and wishing she was.

As she pulled into a space in front of the sub shop, Katie couldn't help noticing how few cars were parked there. Usually on a Friday night the lot would be jammed and bodies would be spilling out the front door. She guessed she was going to be the only customer. Once inside, Katie found she was wrong, but not by much. She quickly counted four heads sticking out over the tops of booths in the back — not exactly a huge crowd. Katie ordinarily would have chosen a table near the back, too — it was where her friends always sat — but tonight the windows at the front of the shop were open, so after her milk shake arrived she took it to a stool looking right out over the sidewalk.

She sipped the cold shake slowly. Too chocolatey, not enough coffee, she thought critically. Oh well. She twisted on her stool, watching the cars go by. The evening breeze touched her through the open window. Katie had a sudden sense of spring, of spring teetering on the brink of summer. It was almost as if, for a second, she could feel time passing, the seasons changing. The feeling made her sad. Another school year was almost over, her last year at Kennedy High School, and where was she? What had brought her here to this moment? What was going to happen next?

Well, she knew what had brought her to the sub

shop: no date on prom night. Breaking up with Greg. Katie winced. She didn't even like to *think* those words, and saying them out loud was even more painful. Of all the traumas and changes she'd gone through these last six months, that was the worst. She supposed everything all tied in together, though. Being jealous of Roxanne, breaking her leg, blaming the accident on Greg and the other boys, missing gymnastics, cutting herself off from her friends, getting into trouble with Torrey Easton — one thing had led to another, then led to yet another. In the end, she was lucky. She'd caught herself before the damage of her depression had gone too deep. Her leg was better and she was back in gymnastics. She still had her friends, who'd always been unquestioningly supportive. But she'd lost Greg. She'd driven him away from her with all her might just when she needed him the most. And now that the school year was almost over, it was really too late for them.

Katie drained her milk shake, willing herself not to get teary. She already had a feeling she'd be crying herself to sleep tonight — she didn't want to start now! When she slipped off her stool to take her paper cup to the trash, she glanced toward the rear of the restaurant again. The four heads were still there, three chatting in one booth, the other alone.

Wait a minute. Katie froze halfway to the garbage can. That one head was facing away from her, but it looked awfully familiar. The way the thick, blond-streaked sandy hair curled just a little at the back of the neck, the angle of the ears . . .

He wasn't sitting with his usual straight-backed posture, in fact, his broad shoulders were set in an uncharacteristic slump, but Katie would know Greg anywhere. *What is he doing here?* she thought, bewildered. She would have banked on him having a date to the prom. Dozens of girls at Kennedy would have been deliriously happy to go with him, even if he was rumored to still be on the rebound from his break-up with Katie.

But as Katie stared at the back of Greg's head she realized that most likely he was at the sub shop for the same reason she was, doing the same thing she was. Even from here he looked kind of down. She threw away her cup and then hesitated. She and Greg hadn't talked in weeks. Could she even bring herself to walk over to his booth and just say "hi"? But she knew if she didn't she'd never forgive herself.

She pushed her hands in the pockets of her shorts and strode purposefully toward Greg, stopping just long enough to pop a few quarters in the jukebox and pick out some lively tunes. *Moral support*, she told herself. A few more steps and she was standing only a couple of inches away from Greg, her heart beating like a drum solo. She swallowed, her throat dry as cotton, and said in a small voice, "Do you mind if I sit with you?"

Greg looked up quickly from the straw wrapper he'd been crumpling. His cheeks went pale with surprise and then red with pleasure. When he smiled broadly at her, Katie knew she'd been right to come over.

"Katie! Sure, have a seat." She slid into the booth across from him and returned his smile.

They stared at one another for a long moment. It had been so long since she'd been this close to Greg, looked right into his eyes, heard his voice when it wasn't through a microphone. She was surprised to see he hadn't changed; she felt about a million years older. Greg snapped out of his trance first. He half-rose, his green eyes still glued to her brown ones. "Can I get you anything?" he asked.

"No, thanks." Katie patted her stomach. "One mocha milk shake a night is my limit!" She smiled wryly. "Don't be surprised if I'm hungry for onion rings in a little while, though."

Greg laughed and there was another brief stretch of silence. Then he cleared his throat. "So," he said, making an effort to sound casual, "it's been a while, huh?"

Katie nodded. "Yeah," she agreed. She dropped her eyes. "It really has."

"I was hoping I'd get a chance to thank you," he continued, still sounding a little bit shy. "For coming to the convention. I saw you there and it . . . it meant a lot to me. Really."

"I'm glad." Katie raised her eyes and they were glowing. "I noticed you at all my meets. *That* meant a lot to *me*."

He grinned. "I'm glad." There was another awkward pause. It struck Katie how hard it was to have a conversation with someone you used to be on intimate terms with but weren't any longer. She and Greg used to talk every day. They talked about their classes, their sports, what they'd had for breakfast, what they thought about this, how they felt about that. It had all been so immediate; they'd been completely in touch and up-to-date. And now there was such a strange distance between them, a lot wider than just a couple of feet of scarred wooden tabletop. The only subjects open to them were the general news items you talked about with casual acquaintances.

Well, it's better than nothing, she decided. I might as well make the most of it. She tucked her feet up under her and leaned her elbows on the table. "The convention was really something!" she observed, a little too brightly. "I don't think anyone expected it to be quite that exciting."

Greg shook his head. "I know, it was really out of hand. I was wondering for a while there what in heck I was doing running for office in the first place! It wasn't a lot of fun standing on that stage waiting to get shot down, I can tell you."

"Well, you handled it really well," Katie told him sincerely. "And besides, you know perfectly well why you ran!" she added, teasing. " 'Cause you'll be the best president J.F.K. High has seen since . . . Chris Austin!" Katie's eyes sparkled mischievously as she referred to the girl Greg had dated before he went out with her.

Greg laughed. "As student body presidents go, she wasn't too shabby," he remembered. "I guess I don't mind being compared to her."

"Not many people would. And by the way, congratulations on winning the election today!"

"Thanks," Greg said. "I was pretty psyched." He paused, coiling the straw wrapper around one of his fingers. "But, hey, what about you? You deserve some congratulations yourself. You're looking pretty good on the old balance beam these days!"

Katie was pleased but unconvinced. "Do you really think so? I'm not sure. I feel sort of like I've plateaued, only nowhere near the top."

"No, you're still improving," Greg said with certainty. "You'll get there."

"Thanks for the vote of confidence."

"Anytime." He crumpled the straw wrapper and tossed it into the ash tray, then leaned back in his seat. "Speaking of improvement," he continued, "that Stacy Morrison has really come a long way in a short time."

"You really think so?" This time Katie's voice was out-and-out enthusiastic. "You know, I've been coaching her on the side," she confided proudly.

"I noticed." Greg grinned. "You can definitely see some of that famous Katie Crawford kick in her these days!"

Katie shrugged, a faint blush stealing across her face. "For a while I wasn't sure if there was any of that stuff still around," she confessed.

"It was always there." Greg's gaze was intense. "You've still got it."

There was another pause while Katie and Greg merely looked at each other. In a way Katie almost thought they could say more with their eyes than with words. But after not talking for so long neither of them was entirely comfortable with silence. Greg broke it this time. "Penny for your thoughts," he asked playfully after a minute.

Katie raised an eyebrow. "You really want them?"

His voice grew serious. "Yeah. I do."

Her smile was rueful. "I was thinking how I'd imagined so many times . . ." she began, looking down at her hands resting on the table so she could hide her eyes behind the thick curtain of her bangs, "I imagined what the big night of my senior prom would be like." Her laugh was dry and distanced. "I never imagined *this.*"

Greg laughed, too. "Ditto."

"I mean, I certainly imagined spending the evening with you," she continued, keeping her voice matter-of-fact. "But at the dance, not the sub shop."

Greg sighed. "I know."

Katie narrowed her eyes at him, curious. "Why didn't you go to the prom with some other girl?"

He thought for a moment. "Same reason you're not there with another guy?" he guessed quietly.

Katie gave him a half-smile instead of an answer. There was another silence, longer but somehow lighter than the others had been. Finally Greg reached across the table and took one of Katie's hands. The gesture startled her and warmed her. It seemed like forever since they'd touched. And even though it was only a small touch, it was a deeply important one. Katie had a feeling she'd never forget this moment.

Greg squeezed her hand. "It's so good to talk, Katie."

"I know." She squeezed his hand in return. "I've missed this," she whispered.

"Me, too," he whispered back.

This time neither of them was in a hurry to interrupt the meaningful silence that fell between them. It was enough for both to sit and think. They were friends again and this realization made Katie's heart soar. Maybe their relationship would never go any further, but for now that was okay. They'd talked, and touched. And suddenly missing the prom didn't seem so bad.

When she'd come into the sub shop just an hour earlier, Katie had thought she'd lost something, and she was sure it was too late to ever get it back. She'd felt like she was near the end of something. Now, as she smiled into Greg's deep, caring eyes, she knew that even if it was almost the end of something, of high school anyway, it could also be a beginning.

Roxanne pushed the door of the sub shop open just as three people were walking out. She peeked in without much of her usual boldness. She was afraid of anybody seeing her, but she was equally afraid that she would be the only person there.

Only one booth in the back was occupied. Some consolation, Rox thought bitterly as she sat at another booth as far away as possible. They were probably strangers, who had gotten lost on their way to D.C., or freshmen or sophomores. She was absolutely sure she was the only upperclassman in all of Rose Hill who was not at the prom.

Roxanne stared at a take-out menu even though she wasn't in the least bit hungry. It gave her something to look at and distracted her, for a few seconds at least, from her depressing thoughts.

Could she force down a burger and fries? She'd skipped dinner, which wasn't hard to do at her house on a Friday night. The chances of her socialite mother being home tonight, much less in the mood to cook, were even slimmer than they were on a weeknight. No, she decided. She might as well save the calories for snacking in front of the television later, watching the late-night movie.

She didn't often feel sorry for herself; Rox wasn't the type to sit on the sidelines and let things happen without her. But the prom wasn't something you made happen, she'd come to realize. You couldn't bully the best-looking guy at school into asking you. Not that she would've wanted to go with Greg anyway, in retrospect. Or any of those Kennedy boys. They'd had their chance and nobody got a second one with her. Pride was a slim consolation, though, when you were left sitting alone on the night of the prom.

She looked at the big empty tables surrounding her. She wasn't sure which one was "the crowd's" regular meeting place. She knew one thing, however. The Stevenson crowd had never laid claim to a particular sub shop table and now they never would. They weren't even really a crowd anymore. Frankie and Lily were gone, it looked like even Daniel was on his way out, and Zachary was never much help in the first place. Even though she'd known all those people didn't exactly like her all the time, she'd considered them her friends. Now that they'd let her down, too, she didn't have anybody.

Lost in these bitter thoughts, Roxanne stared at the couple in the far booth. Then she narrowed her green eyes. Those weren't tourists at all. It was Greg and Katie! How could that be? They'd broken up, everyone knew that. Well, it looked like the romance of prom night had gotten the better of them and they were making up again. It was enough to make you sick. Roxanne wished she could feel disgusted at the sight of them, but in reality she only felt sad, and even more lonely than before. She had to be the only person in the world without a boyfriend, without even a friend. At least in the old days she'd always had Frankie. Now all that was left was her family, and they weren't exactly a "family" in the true sense of the word. She couldn't confide in her divorced, disinterested mother, or worse, her delinquent younger brother.

Roxanne clutched the menu tightly with both hands, unable to tear her eyes away from Katie and Greg. The more she watched them — smiling, talking, laughing — the more alone, betrayed, forgotten she felt. This night was too much like too many other recent nights she'd spent by herself, missing out. The whole semester had been that way, ever since she transferred to Kennedy. It looked like the school year would end soon, and she'd still be alone.

She clenched her teeth, trying very hard not to cry. She couldn't give up; that wouldn't get her anywhere. School wasn't over yet. I'll pay them back, she thought. Greg, Katie, Daniel, Frankie — every single one of them! Despite her efforts, a fat tear slid down over one of Roxanne's high cheekbones. I'll pay them back. I will! I will.

Coming soon . . .

Couples #32

PLAYING DIRTY

"What do you want?" Roxanne asked harshly. Vince stood there stiffly, looking terribly serious. "I want to apologize."

Rox stared at him in surprise. "Apologize? You? What are you apologizing for?"

"For taking up so much room in the newspaper," Vince explained. "I guess I talked too much. If I hadn't there probably would have been room for your interview."

"I'll bet," Roxanne muttered sarcastically.

Vince didn't seem to pick up on her tone. "Honestly, Roxanne," he said sincerely, "it wasn't right that your name was left out. And I'm sure those guys feel really awful about it."

Roxanne's mouth dropped open. Was this guy for real? If he believed what he was saying, he must be even more dense than she'd expected.

Then it dawned on her. Maybe Vince didn't know her history, about how she'd used Jonathan and Eric and Greg. Maybe he didn't know anything about the Kennedy-Stevenson feud she'd created.

It was all becoming clear now, Vince was a wide-eyed innocent, a babe in the woods.

Too bad he was also a dork. And Roxanne was in no mood to deal with dorks — even sincere ones.

"Just leave me alone, okay?" She turned away from him. Just as she did, a hot, dry gust of wind blew a bit of dusty dirt in her eye. As her eye started to sting, she covered it with her hand.

"Are you all right?" Vince asked. Roxanne was aware that Vince was watching her. "Are you okay?" he asked again. That stiff, polite look was gone. There was a serious concern on his face; real sympathy. She realized with a jolt that Vince thought she was crying!

So Vince thought she was upset about the way the crowd had treated her. Well maybe she could use his concern to her advantage. She turned away from him as if she were ashamed for him to see her tears, and put a hand to her eyes. As Vince placed a tentative, comforting hand on her shoulder, Rox began planning feverishly.